喚醒你的英文語感！

Get a Feel for English !

4週商英致勝企畫

PRESENTATION
ENGLISH

簡報英文

作者◎劉培均　審閱◎Quentin Brand

身處全球化時代，英語力即職場致勝關鍵！

我在台灣擔任英語講師二十多年，許多學生和客戶告訴我，他們在進入職場後才意識到，無論規模大小，亦無關外商企業或高科技貿易公司，良好的英語能力對本身的職務都扮演著舉足輕重的關鍵，出色的英語能力能帶來相對大的競爭優勢是無庸置疑的，然而卻都爲時已晚——因爲開始工作之後，才發現根本沒有完整的時間進修英語。早知道當初在學校裡上英文課時，就應該更認眞學習云云。

和爲了通過考試而研讀英語者不同，與其鑽研文法，上班族所需要的是立即有用的“Real English”。事實上，上班族每天處理的事務大多是雷同的。例如，打電話給同僚、廠商或顧客詢問或確認事項；出席會議討論和解決問題；發表簡報以展示新產品或報告執行成果等。而在這些情境之下，使用的語言範圍非常小，其實是相當易於學習和應用的。

「上班族週末充電課」系列書籍旨在有限的時間之內，幫助商務人士以有效率的方式提高英語水準，其中所介紹的文法詞彙之基本用法，以及作者精挑細選的語句，涵蓋電話、會議到簡報所包含的各種商務情境，都能讓上班族立即派上用場。本系列的整體規劃亦恰到好處，讀者能夠在四個星期內完成架構完整的學習。以本書《簡報英文》來說，在快速提升英語力之餘，也有助於理解一個成功的英語簡報應如何開始、說明和結尾等。另外，附加的 MP3 則收錄了全書所有例句，是培養聽力的重要工具——練習聽力的同時，口說表達能力也會同步提升。

總而言之，這個系列對於那些還沒有學習商務英語的人而言，是一個很好的開始，而對那些已經在工作中使用英語但需要一些改進的人來說，則是一個簡明扼要的複習。我眞誠地推薦它。

Quentin Brand

願能成為各位商務英語能力養成的基礎

常從任職於大企業的朋友們口中聽到的一件事，就是憑藉 900 分以上的 TOEIC 成績進公司的職員們，在眞正的英語會議上連一句簡單的商用會話都說不出來，讓他們驚訝不已。

隨著自由貿易協定 (FTA) 讓市場開放的同時，外國企業加快了進入韓國市場的腳步，公司內部使用英語的頻率也變高，讓英語不再是選項而變成必要條件。另外，也有很多企業是內部就有派遣到韓國來工作的員工，讓公司內用英語進行會議、簡報、電話通話、電子郵件的情形變成日常工作的一部分。

如今上班族需要的不再是 TOEIC 成績與死硬的文法知識，而是能將實務所需的英語流暢地說出口，並能有邏輯地傳達自己想法的溝通能力。

本書內容包含「商務簡報」中常會用到的核心句型，以實際簡報爲模型，依主題整理出從簡報開始，到結束之後問答的各種情境，而除了 96 組個別狀況中實用的例句之外，更嚴選收錄了可替換的其他說法。因此，只要按部就班地掌握本書內容，就能熟知英語簡報必備的表達方式，以及進行簡報所需要的程序。

如果已經下定決心要征服商務英語，就認眞地研讀本書吧！四週之後，你就會發現，在內心充實的同時，英語實力也將有大幅進步。

最後，讓我在此感謝協助完成本書的同僚 —— Howat Labrum 教授、Chris Vanden Brook 教授和 Darakwon 出版社編輯部，同時將感謝與榮耀獻給出版準備過程中一直與我同在的上帝。謹以喜悅的心情，將本書獻給在這塊土地上不分日夜辛勤工作的所有產業戰士們，以及學習商務英語的各位讀者。

劉培均

讓商務溝通更有效果的

商務簡報英語週末特訓

〉〉**匯集所有英語簡報進行中之核心表達方式！**

- 96 個必備句型

收錄從簡報開始到結束的問答過程中可以運用的句型、句子，以及可活用來替換的各種說法，讓讀者毫無負擔地一次習得四百多種高頻例句。

- 4 週變大師

為了讓平常忙到幾乎無暇好好休息的上班族可以在短時間內掌握近百種商務簡報必備表達方式，本書特別將內容劃分為 4 堂週末課程，讀者僅需撥出星期六和星期日各兩個小時，集中時間精力研讀各兩堂課即可見效。

- 融入人物角色提升學習樂趣

本書特別設計插畫角色幫助記憶，包含利用週末接受商務英語特訓的上班族，以及名為 Kate 的女老師，讓容易流於單調的英語學習過程變得較為有趣，並增添臨場感，各位讀者不妨以像是在接受家教一般，和書中角色一起練習。

〉〉本書附贈之 CD 收錄全書 Key Expressions 所有精選例句及隨堂測驗、複習之簡報內容，檔案格式為 MP3 檔。由專業外籍配音員錄製，時間約 77 分鐘，容量約 106 MB。

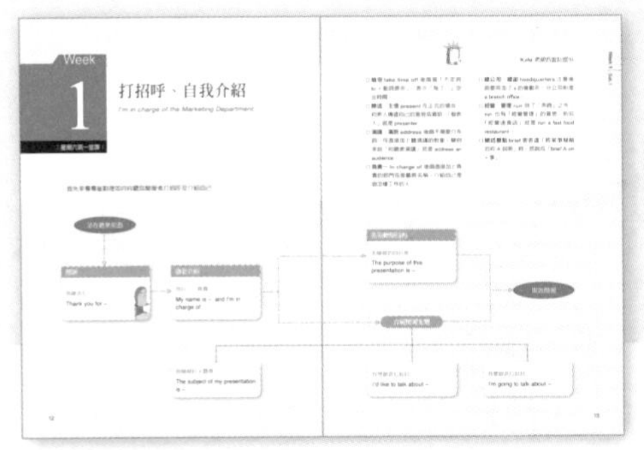

“上課前”

流程圖與重點提示

將該課程中所學到的內容一目了然地整理成流程圖，再搭配 Kate 老師傳授的重點詞彙，讓學習變得更為順暢。

“這個一定要注意”

簡報發表 **Key Expressions 6**

讓讀者熟悉各情況下一定會使用到的 6 種表達方式，還包括淺顯易懂的說明、替換用法，以及實用的商務 TIPS。

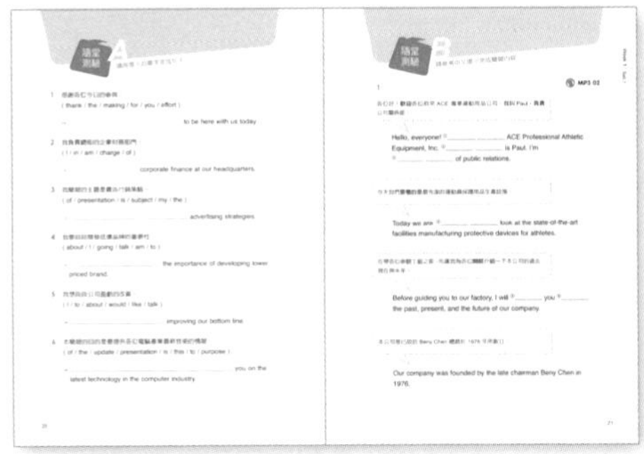

“檢視學過的表達方式”

隨堂測驗

在每堂課之後透過簡短的「隨堂測驗」來驗收前面已經學過的表達方式。

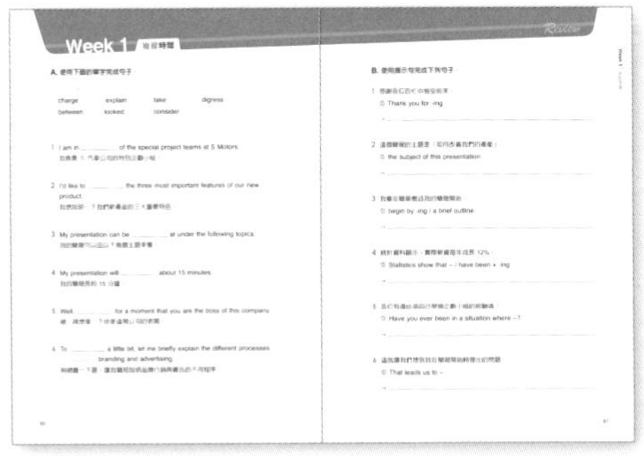

“確實吸收內化”

複習時間

在結束每週末的課程之後，利用以實際商務情境為基礎所設計的句子及段落填空做課後練習。

4週英語週末特訓 Plan

星期六

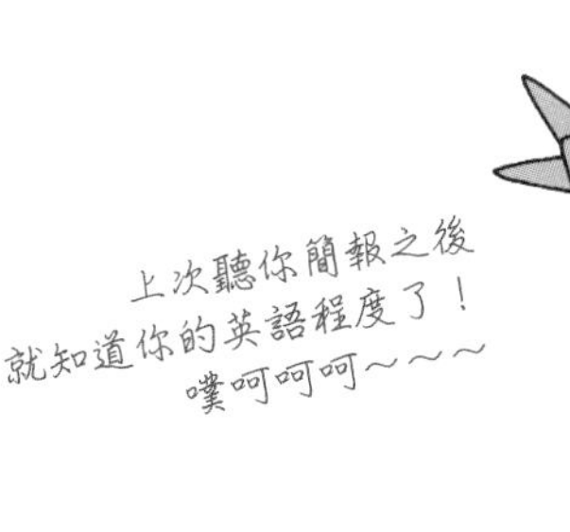
上次聽你簡報之後
就知道你的英語程度了！
噗呵呵呵～～～

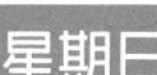

星期日

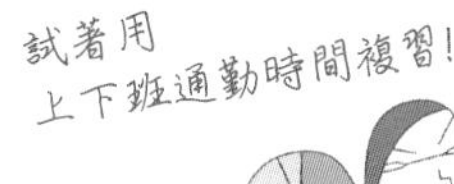
試著用
上下班通勤時間複習！

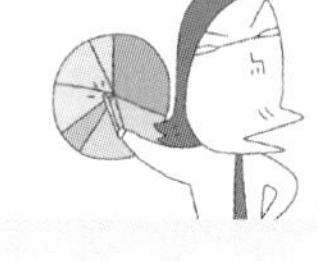

Cheer up!

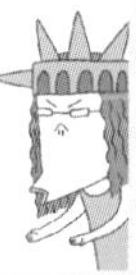

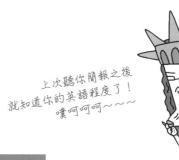

為了有一天能成為英語簡報的達人，
就連公司主管都用這本書來上家教！

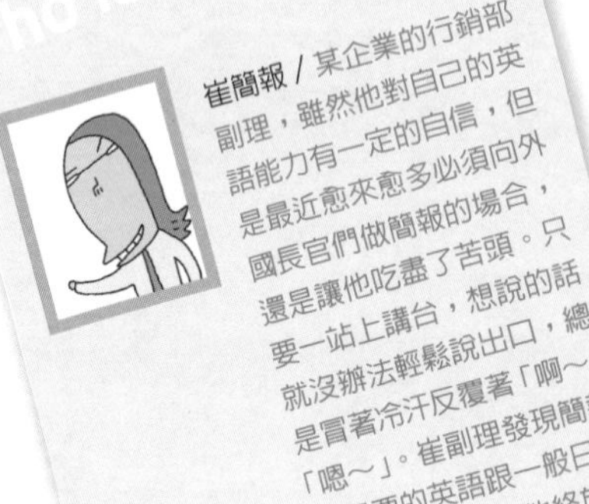

Who is he?

崔簡報／某企業的行銷部副理，雖然他對自己的英語能力有一定的自信，但是最近愈來愈多必須向外國長官們做簡報的場合，還是讓他吃盡了苦頭。只要一站上講台，想說的話就沒辦法輕鬆說出口，總是冒著冷汗反覆著「啊～」「嗯～」。崔副理發現簡報所需要的英語跟一般日常溝通不同，於是他終於向 Kate 伸手求援。

Who is she?

Kate Kim／有著女神外貌的才女兼吃貨。身為華僑第三代的她被紐約的分公司派到台灣，成為那些因英語而苦惱的「英痴」們的家教名師，最喜歡讓人在高級餐廳請吃飯，受過她指點的許多商務人士都在國際舞台上變成英語高手。

Week 1

開始篇

Week 1

打招呼、自我介紹

I'm in charge of the Marketing Department.

｜星期六第一堂課｜

〉〉首先來看看崔副理如何向聽取簡報者打招呼及介紹自己。

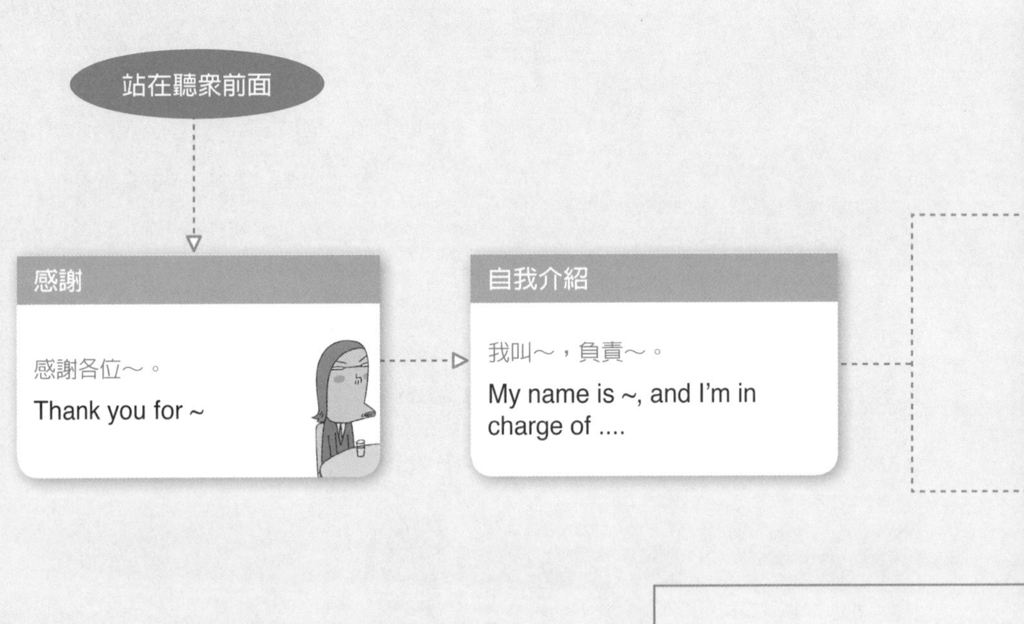

站在聽衆前面
感謝
感謝各位～。
Thank you for ~
自我介紹
我叫～，負責～。
My name is ~, and I'm in charge of ....
我簡報的主題是～。
The subject of my presentation is ~.

Kate 老師的重點提示

- □ **抽空 take time off** 後面接「不定詞 to ＋動詞原形」，表示「為了～」空出時間。
- □ **陳述、主張 present** 在正式的場合，向眾人傳達自己的意見或資訊，「發表人」就是 presenter。
- □ **演講、演說 address** 後面不需要介系詞，可直接加上聽演講的對象，舉例來說「向聽眾演講」就是 address an audience。
- □ **負責～ in charge of** 後面直接加上負責的部門或是職務名稱，介紹自己是做怎樣工作的人。
- □ **總公司、總部 headquarters** 注意後面要用加了 s 的複數形，分公司則是 a branch office。
- □ **經營、管理 run** 除了「奔跑」之外，run 也有「經營管理」的意思，例如「經營速食店」就是 run a fast food restaurant.。
- □ **簡述要點 brief** 要表達「將某事簡略的向 A 說明」時，就說成「brief A on ＋事」。

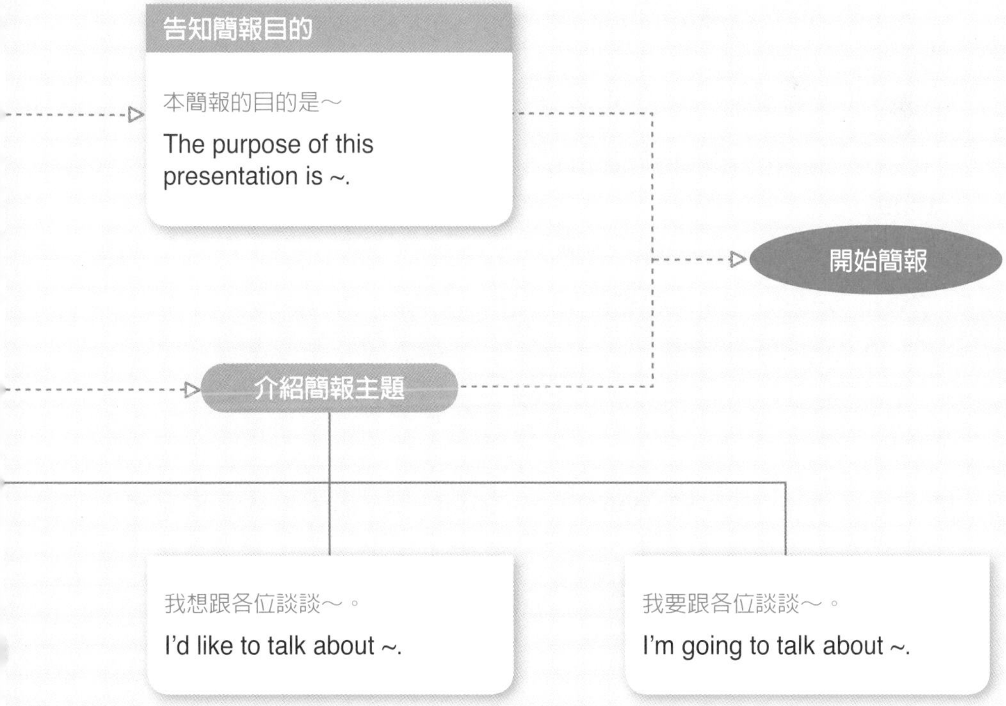

告知簡報目的

本簡報的目的是～

The purpose of this presentation is ~.

開始簡報

介紹簡報主題

我想跟各位談談～。

I'd like to talk about ~.

我要跟各位談談～。

I'm going to talk about ~.

Key Expressions 6

在開始進行簡報前必須先介紹發表者及簡報的目的。以下是成功的簡報在開場時需要處理的事項，以及適當的英語表現方法。

您好，
久仰大名。
喂！相親是
在那一桌啦！
沒睡醒
是吧！

MP3 01

01 Thank you for making the effort to be here with us today.

感謝各位今日的參與。

在簡報的一開始要先向在場者打招呼，可以表示很高興見到大家，也可以感謝在場者的參與。若是正式的場合，可能會由主持人來介紹發表人，在這種情況下，就可以向主持人表示感謝。

表達感謝

- Thank you for taking time off from your busy schedule to be with us today.
  感謝各位百忙中抽空前來參加。
- Thank you for giving me this opportunity to address you today.
  感謝給我這個向各位報告的機會。
- Thank you for the wonderful introduction, Chairman Kim.
  感謝您的精彩介紹，金主席。

Thank you for ... 後面要加上名詞或是動名詞。

›› 還有這樣的表現方式

It's an honor to have the opportunity to address such a distinguished audience.
非常榮幸有機會能對如此優秀的聽衆做演講。

Thank you for being with us.
感謝各位的參與。（比較不正式的說法）

02 My name is Kate Kim, and I am in charge of the Marketing Department.

我叫金凱特，負責行銷部門。

打完招呼之後就要自我介紹。在介紹自己前，可用 Let me start by saying just a few words about my own background.（首先讓我簡單介紹一下我的背景。）或是 For those of you who don't know me, let me introduce myself.（為了在場不認識我的人，讓我介紹一下自己。）這些語句來開頭。

介紹職務

- I am in charge of corporate finance at our headquarters.
  我負責總部的企業財務部門。
- I am in charge of running this exhibition.
  我負責這次的展覽。
- I am in charge of the special project teams at S Motors.
  我在 S 汽車公司負責特別專案小組。

›› 還有這樣的表現方式

I am responsible for product design.
我負責產品設計。

I am the marketing manager for LK Electronics.
我在 LK 電子擔任行銷經理。

I work for KTE Communications.
我在 KTE 電信公司工作。

部門名稱
海外行銷部：Overseas Marketing Department
企劃部：Planning Department
特別專案組：Special Projects Team
產品開發組：Product Development Team
研究開發部：Research and Development (R&D) Department
會計部：Accounting Department
設計部：Design Department

03 The subject of my presentation is advertising strategies.

我簡報的主題是廣告行銷策略。

簡報的主題一開始就必須講得很清楚。subject（主題）這個字可以用 focus（重點）、topic（主題）或 title（題目）來替換。另外，若是較為輕鬆、不正式的場合，也可以用 talk 來取代 presentation。

說明簡報主題 ①

- The subject of my presentation is how to improve our productivity.
  我簡報的主題是如何提升產能。
- The subject of my presentation is how to avoid sexual harassment in the workplace.
  我簡報的主題是如何避免職場性騷擾。
- The subject of my presentation is how we can increase our market share in China.
  我簡報的主題是如何提高在中國市場的占有率。

〉〉還有這樣的表現方式

The topic of my presentation is an analysis of third quarter earnings.
我簡報的主題是第三季收益的分析。

04 I am going to talk about the importance of developing lower priced brands.

我要談談開發低價品牌的重要性。

如 03 所示範的，這種以名詞片語 (The subject of this presentation) 開始的句子語感較為生硬，會讓氣氛變得較為緊張，所以若想要用稍微沒那麼正式的表現方式，可以以對話中常出現的 I am going to ~ 來起頭。

說明簡報主題 ②

- I am going to present a new theory in semiconductor engineering.
  我要介紹一種新的半導體工程理論。

- I am going to brief you on the origins of the computer industry.
  我要跟各位簡略介紹一下電腦產業的起源。

- I am going to update you on some new marketing strategies.
  我要提供各位一些新行銷策略的訊息。

be going to 跟 will 一樣表示未來，但是語感稍有不同。如果是已經立定的計畫與決定，或是想要表現發言者強烈的意圖，就用 be going to，如果只是發言者當下所做的決定，就要用 will。

›› 還有這樣的表現方式

I am delighted to introduce our new product, SN5.
很高興能介紹我們的新產品 SN5。

I am honored to have the opportunity to introduce our new product.
很榮幸能有機會介紹我們的新產品。

05 I'd like to talk about improving our bottom line.

我想談談公司盈虧的改善。

would like to ～ 有「想要～」的意思，是表達自己意圖時很常用的句型，用法上比較沒有那麼正式。

說明簡報主題 ③

- I'd like to talk to you today about the state-of-the-art commercial product design.
  我今天想跟各位談談最先進的商業產品設計。
- I'd like to explain the three most important features of our new product.
  我想說明我們新產品最重要的三項特點。
- I'd like to share our sales data from the last five years.
  我想分享一下我們過去五年的銷售資料。

›› 還有這樣的表現方式

As you know, **I am here today to show** why we have to downsize.
如各位所知，我今天來是要說明我們為何需要縮編。

Let me talk about profit-sharing plans.
讓我來談談利潤分享計畫。

就算要發言的是自己，有時候也會用 Let's ~ 取代 Let me ~ 來開始句子，這樣可以讓聽眾覺得較有親切感。

06 The purpose of this presentation is to inform you about the U.S. market.

本簡報的目的是要提供各位美國市場的訊息。

簡報題目和主題的介紹是 “what”，也就是告知聽眾將要傳達怎樣的訊息；簡報目的則是 “why”，也就是告知聽眾為何要傳達這些訊息。這個句子裡的 purpose 也可以替換成 goal 或是 aim。

告知簡報的目的

- The purpose of this presentation is to explain our position in the deal.
  本簡報的目的是要解釋我們在這次交易中的立場。
- The purpose of this presentation is to update you on the latest technology in the computer industry.
  本簡報的目的是要提供各位電腦產業最新技術的情報。
- The purpose of this presentation is to clarify some points made at our last meeting.
  本簡報的目的是要澄清上次會議的幾個要點。

›› 還有這樣的表現方式

This presentation should serve as the background to recent trends in IT.
本簡報可以作為資訊科技業最新趨勢的背景。

This talk is designed to act as a springboard for developing a new product.
本簡報就是設計來作為新產品開發的跳板。

act 是「作為～角色」的意思。

隨堂測驗 A

請用提示的單字完成句子。

1 感謝各位今日的參與。
(thank / the / making / for / you / effort)

→ ________________ to be here with us today.

2 我負責總部的企業財務部門。
(I / in / am / charge / of)

→ ________________ corporate finance at our headquarters.

3 我簡報的主題是廣告行銷策略。
(of / presentation / is / subject / my / the)

→ ________________ advertising strategies.

4 我要談談開發低價品牌的重要性。
(about / I / going / talk / am / to)

→ ________________ the importance of developing lower priced brand.

5 我想談談公司盈虧的改善。
(I / to / about / would / like / talk)

→ ________________ improving our bottom line.

6 本簡報的目的是要提供各位電腦產業最新技術的情報。
(of / the / update / presentation / is / this / to / purpose)

→ ________________ you on the latest technology in the computer industry.

B 請參考中文提示完成簡報內容。

MP3 02

1

各位好！**歡迎**各位前來 ACE 專業運動用品公司。**我叫** Paul，**負責**公共關係部。

Hello, everyone! ①________ ________ ACE Professional Athletic Equipment, Inc. ②________ ________ is Paul. I'm ③________ ________ of public relations.

今天我們**要看的是**最先進的運動員保護用品生產設施。

Today we are ④________ ________ look at the state-of-the-art facilities manufacturing protective devices for athletes.

在帶各位參觀工廠之前，先讓我為各位**簡略介紹一下**本公司的過去、現在與未來。

Before guiding you to our factory, I will ⑤________ you ⑥________ the past, present, and the future of our company.

本公司是已故的 Beny Chen 總裁於 1976 年所創立。

Our company was founded by the late chairman Beny Chen in 1976.

2

各位先生、女士早安，**我是**金凱特，**負責**企劃部。

Good morning, ladies and gentlemen! ①________ ________ Kate Kim, and I am ②________ for the Planning Department.

本簡報的**目的是要**讓各位知道為何要投資這個事業計畫。

The ③________ ________ this presentation is ④________ show you why we have to invest in this business plan.

3

各位午安，謝謝各位**前來參與**。我叫林秀賢，**負責**策略行銷部。

Good afternoon, everyone. Thank you ①________ being with us. My name is Su Hyun Lin. I am in charge of ②________ ________.

今天我**要**談談開發我們日常消費用品之新品牌的必要性。

Today, I'm ③________ ________ talk about the need to make a new brand for our daily consumer goods.

Bonus

必要的英語簡報成功策略

這是正式還是非正式的簡報？

簡報最重要的是用詞的選擇。如果是在公司重要人士面前做簡報，或是拜訪其他機關團體，最好用較為正式的詞彙。不過如果是熟悉的對象，則不需要太過正式，可以選用較平易近人的詞彙來緩和氣氛。一般來說，非正式的表現方式會讓聽取對象感到較為舒服。

簡報的起頭絕對禁止浪費時間！

簡報的起頭只需要打招呼 (greeting)、介紹發言者 (introducing presenter)、介紹簡報主題 (subject) 和目的 (purpose)、說明所需時間 (length) 及之後的提問時間 (a question-and-answer session)。特別是外國人大都習慣於 Let's get down to business（進入正題）的文化，過於冗長的前言只會讓人感到不舒服。

說話要充滿熱情、簡單明瞭！

檢查一下自己在簡報裡用的句子以確定這些單字和句子是不是夠清楚簡潔，而且要使用適當的講述 (deliver) 速度跟肢體語言 (body language，比方說 eye-contact)。簡報時特別要好好地傳達出自己對這些內容的自信 (confidence) 與熱情 (enthusiasm)。

隨堂測驗 A

1 Thank you for making the effort 2 I am in charge of
3 The subject of my presentation is 4 I am going to talk about
5 I would like to talk about 6 The purpose of this presentation is to update

隨堂測驗 B

1 ① Welcome to ② My name ③ in charge ④ here to ⑤ brief ⑥ on
2 ① I am ② responsible ③ purpose[aim / goal] of ④ to
3 ① for ② strategic marketing ③ going to

Week 1

傳達概要＆說明所需時間

My presentation will take about 15 minutes.

｜星期六第二堂課｜

》跟著崔副理一起來看看向聽眾說明簡報概要和所需時間的過程吧！

說明簡報開始

我將從～開始。

I'll begin by ~.

說明簡報的概要

我的簡報可以分成～部分。

My presentation can be divided into ~.

有 2 個小主題時

一個是～，另外一個是～。

- One is ~, the other is ~.
- First is ~, last is ~.

有 3 個小主題時

第一是～，接著是～，然後是～。

- First ~, next ~, and then ~.
- Firstly ~, then ~, finally ~.
- Firstly ~, secondly ~, lastly ~.

Kate 老師的重點提示

□ **概略、概要 overview** 意指簡略地說明某個主題，「做概略說明～」就是 give an overview of ~，也可以用 outline 取代 overview。

□ **看看 take[have] a look at** 單純用眼睛看的狀況用動詞 see，如果是集中注意力看著某一點的話就用 look。

□ **觀察、注目、觀察後的意見 observation** make an observation about ~ 就是「對～做出評述」。

□ **花費（～時間）take** 要說明簡報大約會花費多少時間時，可用「My presentation will take + 時間」這樣的句型。

□ **自由、無拘無束 free** 要表達「請隨時隨意地～」時，可用 feel free to ~ 這樣的命令句型，告知對方有問題或是需要幫忙時盡量提出，也可以換成 Don't hesitate to ~。

□ **分成～ be divided into** 除了這個句型之外，要表示分成幾個項目時，也可以說 be broken down into。

□ **告知～、說 inform / talk** 向他人說明某種訊息或是計畫時，可用「inform 人 of 訊息」或是「talk 人 about 訊息」。

告知所需時間

我的簡報長約～。

My presentation will take about ~.

說明提問相關事項

如果各位有問題的話，請隨時發問。

If you have any questions, feel free to ask them.

最後會有提問的時間。

There will be time for questions at the end.

有 4 個小主題時

第一是～，第二是～，第三是～，最後是～。

- First ~, second ~, third ~, last ~.
- The first item is ~, the second ~, the third ~, the last ~.

Key Expressions 6

在簡報開始時必須簡單地概述接下來的簡報方向，這樣聽者才可以更容易掌握簡報的核心事項。這堂課就要讓大家熟悉概要的說明與告知時間的表現方法。

 MP3 03

01 I will begin by giving you a brief outline of my talk.

我將以介紹我簡報的概要來開始。

在簡報開始時要先點出當天簡報內容的 outline，也就是重點概要，可以用「首先我會以～來開始」做為簡報的開場。另外，在發表過程中持續跟聽眾說明進行方向也是很重要的。

 正式開始簡報

- I will begin by giving you an overview of today's market situation.
  我將從跟各位概述當今的市場狀況開始。
- I will begin by giving a few observations.
  我將從提出幾個觀察所見開始。
- I will begin by bringing you up-to-date on the latest findings on consumer behavior.
  我將從提供各位消費者行為的最新發現開始。

也可以用 start 或是 kick off 來取代 begin。

》還有這樣的表現方式

I'm going to start with the background of my downsizing proposal.
我會以我的縮編提案背景開始。

Then I will go on to talk about some strategies to win back our market share.
接著我會談到幾個贏回市場占有率的策略。

My presentation can be divided into three sections.

我的簡報可以分為三個部分。

敘述簡報概要時，最好能按照主題或是階段別來細分每個部分，說明接下來要展開的內容方向。這樣的概要格式不只能顯示簡報準備的系統化與細膩感，更可以讓聽衆輕易理解並跟上簡報的內容。

說明簡報的概要

- My presentation can be divided into four subjects.
  我的簡報可以分為四個主題。
- My presentation can be looked at under the following topics.
  我的簡報可以由以下這幾個主題來看。
- My presentation can be broken down into the following headings.
  我的簡報可以細分成下面幾個標題。

›› 還有這樣的表現方式

I have separated my presentation **into** the following headings.
我將我的簡報分成下面幾個主題。

當被關注的對象不是行為的主體，而是接受該行為的事物或人物時，就要用被動式的句型。像下面的例句，因為關注的焦點是簡報被如何處理，而不是誰對簡報做了什麼，所以用被動式會比較好。

I have divided my presentation into four parts.（主動式）
→ My presentation can be divided into four sections.（被動式）

03 First ..., then ..., and finally ....
Firstly ..., secondly ..., lastly....

第一……，第二……，最後……。

以下是可以用來列舉簡報內容細部項目的詞彙。

有 3 個小主題時

- Firstly, I'll examine overseas markets. Secondly, we will take a look at domestic markets. Finally, I will outline efficient ways to penetrate these markets.
  首先，我會檢視海外市場。其次，我們會看一下國內市場。最後，我會概述一下進入這些市場的有效方式。

- There are three stages involved: first the background, then the present situation, and lastly the prospects for the future.
  一共涉及三個階段：第一是背景，然後是現況，最後是未來的展望。

> There is[are] 用來說明什麼東西「存在」或是「不存在」。(It is ~ 沒有辦法表達這種意思。)

有 4 個小主題時

- I'll describe the four steps involved in developing the idea. They are, first, an overview of our target market; second, the need to make a new logo; third, the strategies for a publicity campaign; and finally, the introduction of TQM.
  我會說明發展這個想法所涉及的四個階段。第一，我們目標市場的概況；第二，創造新商標的必要性；第三，宣傳策略；最後是全面品質管理的導入。

My presentation will take about 20 minutes.

我的簡報長約 20 分鐘。

在說明完簡報的概要之後，就要告知預計將要花費的時間。如果簡報很長而中間會有休息時間的話，這個時候也要告知聽眾。

告知簡報所需時間

也可以用有持續意味的 last 來取代 take。

- My presentation will take only ten minutes of your time.
  我的簡報只會占用各位 10 分鐘時間。
- My presentation will take about 15 minutes.
  我的簡報長約 15 分鐘。
- My presentation will take about one hour, but there will be a ten-minute break in the middle.
  我的簡報長約 1 小時，不過中間會有一段 10 分鐘的休息。

›› 還有這樣的表現方式

※ 也可以再加上下面的句子。

Refreshments will be provided for you during the break.
休息時間會提供各位茶點。

05 If you have any questions, feel free to ask them.

如果各位有問題的話，請隨時發問。

這是關於提問的說明。如果簡報進行中可以隨時發問的話，就用這樣的表現方式來告知。

說明提問相關事項 ①

- Please feel free to ask any questions.
  請隨時提問。

- If you have any questions about this topic, feel free to ask me.
  如果各位對這個主題有任何問題，請隨時提出來問我。

›› 還有這樣的表現方式

Please **interrupt me at any time** if you have any questions.
如果各位有任何問題，請隨時打斷我。

Please **do not hesitate to ask** (any) questions.
有問題的話請不要猶豫，直接問。

06 There will be time for questions at the end.

最後會給各位提問的時間。

這是另一個關於提問的說明。如果簡報過程中想避免聽眾干擾，而希望聽眾在簡報後的提問時間才接受問題的話，可先說 If you have any questions, please save them for the end.（如果各位有任何問題，請留到最後），然後使用下列的表現方式。

說明提問相關事項 ②

- After my presentation, there will be time for questions.
  我的簡報結束後會給各位提問的時間。

- There will be a question-and-answer session after the presentation.
  簡報結束後會有 Q&A 的時間。

- After my presentation, there will be time for questions, which will last ten minutes.
  我的簡報結束後會給各位提問的時間，大約 10 分鐘。

›› 還有這樣的表現方式

I will be happy to answer any questions at the end of my talk.
簡報結束後，我很樂意回答任何問題。

I will try to answer all of your questions after the presentation.
簡報結束後，我會試著回答各位的所有提問。

隨堂測驗 A

請用提示的單字完成句子。

1 我將從跟各位概述當今的市場狀況來開始。
(giving / I / by / you / begin / will)

→ ＿＿＿＿＿, ＿＿＿＿＿＿＿＿＿＿ an overview of today's market situation.

2 我將我的簡報分為四個部分。
(parts / presentation / into / my / four / divided)

→ I have ＿＿＿＿＿＿＿＿＿＿＿＿＿＿＿＿＿＿＿＿.

3 最後，我會概述一下進入這些市場的有效方式。
(finally / ways / I / efficient / outline / will)

→ ＿＿＿＿＿＿＿＿＿＿＿＿＿＿＿ to penetrate these markets.

4 我的簡報長約 20 分鐘。
(take / my / about / will / presentation)

→ ＿＿＿＿＿＿＿＿＿＿＿＿＿＿＿ twenty minutes.

5 如果各位有問題的話，請隨時發問。
(you / any / if / questions / have)

→ ＿＿＿＿＿＿＿＿＿＿＿＿＿, feel free to ask them.

6 我的簡報結束後會給各位提問的時間。
(be / time / for / questions / will / there)

→ After my presentation, ＿＿＿＿＿＿＿＿＿＿＿＿＿＿＿＿＿＿.

隨堂測驗 B

請參考中文提示完成簡報內容。

MP3 04

1

我將我的簡報**分為**三個部分。**首先**，我會報告消費者在超市購買日常消費用品**時**的品牌偏好。

I have ①________ my presentation ②________ three parts.
③________, I will report on consumers' brand preference ④________ they purchase everyday consumer goods at supermarkets.

其次，我會討論台灣頂級超市吸引消費者的品牌策略，**最後**，我將說明為何我們需要開發一個新的品牌。

⑤________, I will discuss Taiwan top supermarkets' branding strategies to appeal to consumers. And ⑥________ I will talk about why we need to develop a new brand.

我的簡報**長約** 30 分鐘，結束之後我很樂意回答**任何**問題。

My talk will take ⑦________ 30 minutes, and I will be happy to answer ⑧________ questions at the end.

2

好，謝謝各位今天**來參加**，我是林敏智，集團重整處長。如各位所知，我來**這裡**是要談談我們企業組織重整的計畫。

OK, thank you for ①________ today. I am Minji Lin, the Group Restructuring Director. As you know, I am ②________ to talk about our plan for restructuring our business organization.

我的簡報可以**細分**成三個部分，**之後**會有 30 分鐘的問答時間。我會以我縮編提案的背景來**開始**。

My talk can be ③________ down into three parts followed ④________ a 30-minutes question-and-answer session. I am going to ⑤________ with the background to my downsizing proposal.

接著，在**第二個**部分，我要談談幾個知名公司的成功重整案例。最後，在我簡報的**最終**部分，我會以提出幾個建議**作為結束**，以便使我們重整的努力可以讓公司與員工雙贏。

Then, in the ⑥________ part, I will go over some successful restructuring cases at big name companies. Finally, in my ⑦________ part, I will ⑧________ with some recommendations to make our restructuring efforts a win-win situation both for our company and the employees.

Bonus

選擇讓簡報有效果的詞彙

使用中性的語言

隨著女性在職場上的活躍，有愈來愈多以往用來形容職務與角色的單字變得中性，比方說商人、實業家本來叫 businessman，現在大多改用 business person 這樣的單字。

同樣的，「總裁」這個字原本叫 chairman，現在也改用 chair-person；「空服員」也從 steward 或是 stewardess 改成 flight attendant。

另外，原本會用 Miss 跟 Mrs. 這兩個字來區分未婚與已婚女性，現在幾乎都改成用 Ms. 來通稱。同時，第三人稱單數代名詞的使用也有類似的狀況，最近的趨勢是盡量不使用 he、she、him、her、his、hers 等這些 sexist language（性別歧視語言）。為了避開區分性別的單字，現在會兩個一起用，或是改用複數的代名詞。

【例】An employer must hire **his or her** secretary.
雇主必須雇用他／她的祕書。

Employers must hire **their** secretaries.
雇主們必須雇用他們的祕書。

隨堂測驗 A

1 I will begin by giving you 2 divided my presentation into four parts
3 Finally, I will outline efficient ways 4 My presentation will take about
5 If you have any questions 6 there will be time for questions

隨堂測驗 B

1 ① divided ② into ③ Firstly[First] ④ when ⑤ Secondly ⑥ finally[lastly] ⑦ about ⑧ any
2 ① coming ② here ③ broken ④ by ⑤ start[begin] ⑥ second ⑦ last ⑧ end

Week

1 有效果的起頭方式

How would you like to market our new product?

| 星期日第一堂課 |

〉〉跟著崔副理一起來看看怎樣的說話方式能引發聽衆的好奇心與注意。

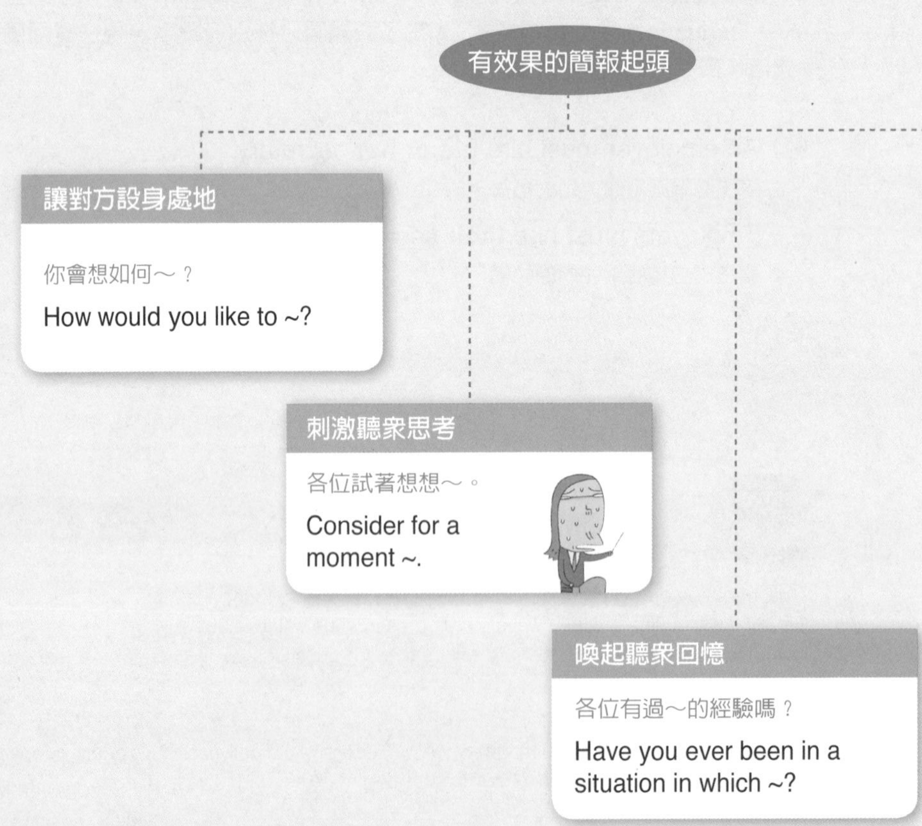

有效果的簡報起頭
讓對方設身處地
你會想如何～？
How would you like to ~?
刺激聽衆思考
各位試著想想～。
Consider for a moment ~.
喚起聽衆回憶
各位有過～的經驗嗎？
Have you ever been in a situation in which ~?

Kate 老師的重點提示

□（如果是你的話）你會怎樣～？ **How would you like to ~?** 可以誘導對方換位思考的表現方式。

□統計、統計資料 **statistics** 要用複數。不過如果是「統計學」就要用單數。

□顯示 **show** 統計資料「顯示～」，英文就是 Statistics show ~。

□考慮 **consider** 後面可加上名詞子句或是動名詞作為受詞。另外，consider for a moment 是指「考慮一下」。

□各位有想過～？ **Have you ever wondered ~?** 詢問經驗時用現在完成式，也就是「Have + 主詞 + ever + 過去分詞～？」這樣的結構。

□認知、了解 **realize** 也就是 become aware of 的意思。

□身處～的狀況 **be in a situation in which ~** 說明狀況時，situation 後面可加上 in which 這樣的關係代名詞結構。

□有多少人知道～？ **How many people realize ~?** 將許多人沒有認知到的重要事實點出來時，可以用這個句子來表達。

引用有公信力的資料

統計資料顯示～。

Statistics show that ~.

說出能讓人驚訝的事實

在場有多少人知道～？

How many people here realize that ~?

誘發聽眾的好奇心

各位有想過～嗎？

Have you ever wondered ~?

Key Expressions 6

簡報正式開始時的起頭方式會決定是否能誘導出聽眾的好奇和興趣，本課將會介紹六個有效果的起頭方式。

MP3 05

01 How would you like to launch your own business?

你會想如何開始你自己的事業？

第一個是換位思考策略，這是指讓聽的人站在簡報發表人的立場思考。簡單來說，就是讓對方換個立場想想「如果是這樣的狀況你會怎麼做？」。

launch 是「著手、開始（事業、計畫、改革等）」的意思，與 start 同義。

使用換位思考策略

- How would you like to market our new product?
  你會想如何行銷我們的新產品？
- How would you like to satisfy consumers' needs?
  你會想如何滿足消費者的需求？
- How would you like to sell the refrigerator to the Eskimos?
  你會想如何賣冰箱給愛斯基摩人？

›› 還有這樣的表現方式

How would you prefer to advertise our new product?
你會想如何幫我們的新產品做廣告？

How would you prefer to improve the welfare of our employees?
你會想如何增進我們員工的福利？

02 Well, consider for a moment where the recent fashion trend is headed.

嗯，請試著想想最近的流行趨勢是往哪個方向。

簡報中最重要的是發表者與聽衆間的互動和交流，也就是 interaction 和 rapport。因此，發表者要注意不能變成單方面的發表，要能誘導跟刺激聽衆的參與才行。

誘導聽衆參與

- Well, consider for a moment what the number one priority in our industry is.
  嗯，請試著想想這個產業最優先需要的是什麼。
- Well, consider for a moment that you are the boss of this company.
  嗯，請試著把自己想成這間公司的老闆。
- Well, consider for a moment the prospects for next year's economy.
  嗯，請試著想想明年的經濟展望。

›› 還有這樣的表現方式

Think for a moment about the positive reactions to our new plan.
請試著想想我們新計畫所帶來的正面反應。

Give some thought to the differences between the new product and the old one.
請試著想想新產品與舊產品之間的差異。

03 Have you ever wondered how the company overcame the obstacles?

各位有想過公司是怎樣克服了困境嗎？

可以丟出與周遭的驚人事件、成功神話、失敗案例等相關的問題讓聽眾產生疑問，聽眾會知道這種問題的答案跟簡報內容有關，而更加集中注意力。

刺激聽眾的求知心

- Have you ever wondered what makes Macau the hottest playground destination?
  各位有想過是什麼讓澳門成為最熱門的旅遊享樂地點嗎？

- Have you ever wondered why we can't be number one in the industry?
  各位有想過為何我們無法變成業界第一嗎？

- Have you ever wondered why the iPhone series achieved such a spectacular success?
  各位有想過為何 iPhone 系列會獲得如此耀眼的成績嗎？

›› 還有這樣的表現方式

Have you ever thought about the interests of our customer?
各位有想過我們顧客的喜好嗎？

Have you ever thought about why the sales of our products are slow?
各位有想過為何我們產品的銷售如此低迷嗎？

04 Statistics show that the US is still ranked first in labor productivity in the world.

統計資料顯示美國的勞動生產力仍居世界第一。

大多數人對統計的客觀與科學性有信心，所以會偏好數據化的統計資料，因此，適當使用與主題相關的統計資料，可以幫助吸引聽眾的注意。

利用有信賴性的統計數據

- Statistics show that American productivity has fallen in recent years.
  統計資料顯示美國的生產力近年來逐漸降低。
- Statistics show that China will be the star of the world's economy in ten years.
  統計資料顯示中國在十年內會成為世界經濟之星。
- Statistics show that Japan has continued its economic recovery.
  統計資料顯示日本的經濟持續在復甦。
- Official statistics show the GDP of our country has been declining by 2% a year.
  官方統計資料顯示我國的國內生產總值一年減少 2%。
- Statistics show that real wages have been increasing by 12% per year.
  統計資料顯示實際薪資每年以 12% 額度增加。

請記得，如果要透過統計資料提供資訊，就一定要給予正確的數字。

05 How many people here realize that even the Internet cannot be immune to censorship?

在場有多少人知道連網路也無法免於被審查？

起頭時提出不太為人所知的驚人事實也可以有效抓住聽眾的注意力。當然，要提出與簡報主題有密切關係的事實才行。

提供驚人事實

- How many people here realize that transfats are doubly bad for the heart?

  在場有多少人知道反式脂肪對心臟的傷害是加倍的？

- How many people here realize that Carl Icahn built his fortune by threatening companies with hostile takeovers?

  在場有多少人知道卡爾 ・ 伊坎是用惡意收購來威脅公司以建立他的財富？

- How many people here realize that the demand for organic foods keeps increasing every year?

  在場有多少人知道有機食品的需求每年都在上升？

›› 還有這樣的表現方式

How many of you realize that a lot of people take regular supplements everyday?

各位當中有多少人知道許多人每天都會食用營養補給品？

06 Have you ever been in a situation in which you had to solve a problem by yourself?

各位有過必須獨自解決問題的經驗嗎？

問聽衆有沒有與主題相關的經驗可以使聽衆比較自己與發表者的經驗，看看二者間有什麼差異進而得到怎樣的教訓，所以這也是引發聽衆興趣的有效方法。

喚起與主題相關的經驗

- Have you ever been in a situation in which you were involved in an argument with a customer?
  各位有過與顧客起衝突的經驗嗎？
- Have you ever been in a situation in which you were pressured to buy a product?
  各位有過被迫買某樣產品的經驗嗎？
- Have you ever been in a situation in which you messed up your assignment?
  各位有過搞砸任務的經驗嗎？

mess up 是指把事情「搞砸」，也就是沒把事情做好的意思。

›› 還有這樣的表現方式

Have you ever been in a situation where you had to negotiate?
各位有過必須與人協商談判的經驗嗎？

Have you ever been in a situation where you had to lead a project team?
各位有過必須自己帶領企劃小組的經驗嗎？

隨堂測驗 A

請用提示的單字完成句子。

1 你會想如何行銷我們的新產品？
(like / to / would / market / how / you)

→ ______________________________ our new product?

2 請試著想想日漸重要的手機內容。
(a / for / consider / the / moment / growing)

→ Well, ______________________________
importance of mobile content.

3 統計資料顯示美國的勞動生產力仍居世界第一。
(first / still / show / the US / ranked / statistics / that / is)

→ ______________________________ in labor
productivity in the world.

4 各位有過必須自己解決問題的經驗嗎？
(have / which / you / a / been / in / ever / in / situation)

→ ______________________________ you had to
solve a problem by yourself?

5 各位有想過為何 iPhone 系列會獲得如此耀眼的成績嗎？
(ever / you / have / why / wondered)

→ ______________________________ the iphone series achieved such
a spectacular success?

6 在場有多少人知道連網路也無法免於被審查？
(here / that / how / many / people / realize)

→ ______________________________ even the Internet cannot be
immune to censorship?

隨堂測驗 B

請參考中文提示完成簡報內容。

MP3 06

1

統計資料顯示，有機食品的消費在過去五年間急速上升。

①________ ________ that the consumption of organic foods has
②________ dramatically over the past five years.

這表示，所謂的健康生活已經成為愈來愈多消費者的首要考量之一，這也告訴我們該在市場上開發並推出怎樣的飲料。

③________ this implies is that the so-called well-being of life is becoming one of the top priorities for more and more consumers. This tells us what ④________ of drinks we have to develop and introduce to the ⑤________.

本日簡報的主題是，「讓我們製造一種可以滿足消費者對健康追求的健康飲料」。

The ⑥________ of today's presentation is "Let's Make a Well-Being Drink Which ⑦________ the Consumer's Desire to Be Healthy."

2

你會想**如何**開始自己的事業？事業成功需要**考慮**哪些要素？

①________ would you like to launch your own business? What elements do you have to ②________ to make your business successful?

首先，你要先**決定**你的主要事業活動是什麼，是製造產品還是提供服務？當然，你需要資金來建立你的事業。

③________, you have to ④________ what your main business activities will be, manufacturing products or selling services? Of course, you need capital to finance your business.

接著，你必須想想如何組織你的事業。你也必須決定要雇用**多少**人。

And ⑤________, you have to think about how to structure your business. You also have to decide how ⑥________ people you are going to employ.

不過，需要考慮的是重要事項**之一**，就是構思自己公司的願景。沒錯吧？本日的簡報**主題**就是在經營事業時公司**願景**的重要性。

But ⑦________ of the most important things to consider is to formulate the vision of your company. Right? The ⑧________ of today's talk is the importance of company ⑨________ in doing business.

成功簡報者的十誡

1. 確實的檢查設備

事前要確實的檢查簡報地點、座位、燈光、音響、投影機、雷射筆等等所有簡報會用到的設備。

2. 熟記起頭的方法

細心的設計起頭的方式，而且要熟記起頭的句子。

3. 直接帶入主題

太過冗長的開場白會讓聽眾覺得無聊，所以必須用一兩句強而有力的開場白來吸引聽眾注意。

4. 與聽眾對話

優秀簡報的要件之一是用對話方式來表達，不斷地向聽眾提問並且做適當的回應。

5. 講話自然

該猶豫的時候就猶豫，該休息的時候就休息，簡報者不是在背台詞的演員。

6. 要懂聽眾

要知道聽眾的慾望、目標與關注點，簡報者要跟聽眾處在同一個水平線上。

7. 要從容地進行

不要因為時間不夠就倉促行事，傳達核心重點時記得要從容緩慢、清晰地傳達。

8. 視覺資料上不要放說明

視覺資料要簡單明瞭，說明也要簡短，重要的是能讓聽眾自己看資料並掌握內容。

9. 對任何問題都開心的接受

要把聽眾的問題當作可以更詳細說明簡報意圖的道具。

10. 結尾要強而有力

簡報的結尾速度要放慢，聲調也要降低，緩慢清晰地講出結論，稍作暫停，然後播放簡報上的結論頁，接著用感謝來結束簡報。

隨堂測驗 A

1 How would you like to market 2 consider for a moment the growing
3 Statistics show that the US is still ranked first 4 Have you ever been in a situation in which
5 Have you ever wondered why 6 How many people here realize that

隨堂測驗 B

1 ① Statistics show ② increased ③ What ④ kind ⑤ market ⑥ title ⑦ Satisfies
2 ① How ② consider ③ First[Firstly] ④ decide ⑤ then ⑥ many ⑦ one ⑧ subject ⑨ vision

Week

1

進行簡報

Let's move on to office security system.

| 星期日第二堂課 |

〉〉跟著崔副理一起看看要如何順暢連結簡報的每個階段。

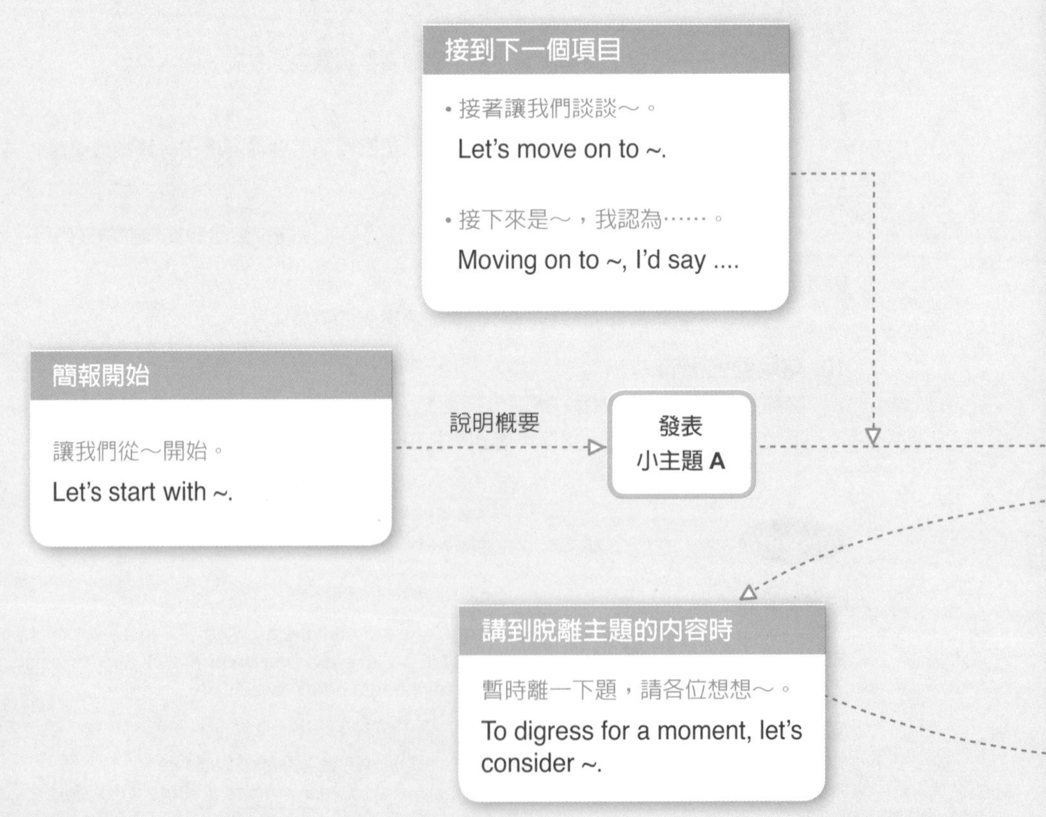

接到下一個項目
• 接著讓我們談談～。
Let's move on to ~.
• 接下來是～，我認為……。
Moving on to ~, I'd say ....
簡報開始
讓我們從～開始。
Let's start with ~.
說明概要
發表
小主題 A
講到脫離主題的內容時
暫時離一下題，請各位想想～。
To digress for a moment, let's consider ~.

Kate 老師的重點提示

□ **以～開始 start with** 用來告訴聽衆你準備以什麼話題來進入正題，也可以用 begin by ~ / kick off by ~ 來表示。

□ **提出（問題、疑問等） raise** 除了「舉起、引起」的意思之外，也有「提出」某種意見或問題的意思，例如 raise a question / raise an issue（提出問題）。

□ **（話題等）離題 digress** 簡報中當有需要提一些與主題無關的話題時，可用 to digress for a moment(暫時離一下題)這樣的表現方式。

□ **導致～出現～的結果 lead ... to ~** 說明「因著某事造成某種結果」的動詞用 lead，也可以用 That leads us to ~ 這樣的句型。

□ **移到 move on to** 用來說明下面將要「移到、換到」下一個主題，turn to 也是一樣的意思，比方說 move on[turn] to the next issue（換到下一個主題）。

□ **將注意力放到～上 focus on** 要講到重要事項或資料時，可以用這個句型來吸引聽衆的注意力，比方說 Let's focus on ~（讓我們把焦點放到～上）。

□ **請各位想想～ Let's consider[think about] ~** 利用這樣的句子來引導聽衆一起思考。

發表
小主題 B

講出結果

這讓我們了解到～。

- That leads us to understand ~.
- Then we come to ~.

回到主題

讓我們回到～的問題上。

Let's go back to the issue of ~.

Key Expressions 6

簡報的主體 (body) 就是用來表現目的與主張的核心部分，讓我們來看看要如何自然連貫簡報的各個部分，以便能有系統地傳達簡報的內容。

MP3 07

01 Let's start with the latest advances in information technology.

讓我們從資訊科技的最新發展開始。

為了讓簡報能維持節奏的順暢，在換到下一個主題或是轉換方向時必須告知聽眾，也就是所謂的 signposting 或是 sequencing。讓我們先看看進入正題的方法：

開始進入正題

- Let's start with the latest development in office technology.
  讓我們從辦公技術的最新發展開始。
- Let's start with the latest trends in teen fashions.
  讓我們從青少年時尚的最新趨勢開始。
- Let's start with a recap of last night's discussion.
  讓我們從概述昨晚的討論開始。

recap 是「重述要點」、「概括」的意思。

›› 還有這樣的表現方式

Let's begin by making a few observations about our sales forecast.
讓我們從評論一下預計銷售量開始。

Let's kick off by taking a look at the recent boom in DMB phones.
讓我們從談談最近 DMB 手機的熱潮開始。

DMB: Digital Multimedia Broadcasting 的意思。

02

Let's move on to office security systems.

接著讓我們談談辦公室保全系統。

當簡報的內容 (body) 分成幾個項目時，可以用以下幾種表現方式來結束一個項目然後接到下一個項目。

接續到下一個項目 ①

- Let's move on to the problem of working with international laborers.
  接著讓我們談談與外勞一起工作的問題。
- Let's move on to our targets for the next five years.
  接著讓我們談談之後五年的目標。
- Let's move on to the issue of minimum wage.
  接著讓我們談談最低工資的問題。

> minimum wage（最低工資）↔ six-figure income 就是「六位數所得」

›› 還有這樣的表現方式

Let's turn now to the results of our effort so far.
現在讓我們接著看看到目前為止我們努力的結果。

Let's direct our attention to the end-of-the-year sales figures.
讓我們接著看看年底的銷售數字。

Let's focus on the latest findings of the market research.
讓我們專注於市場調查的最新發現。

03 Moving on to the issue of saving costs, I want to ask for Mr. Choi's opinion on this first.

接下來是節省費用的問題，我想先聽聽崔先生的意見。

這是另一個可以轉移到下一個項目的表現方式。如果一直用同樣的句型，聽眾會厭煩，所以要懂得活用不同的表現方式。另外，也可以用現在分詞 going 來取代 moving。

接續到下一個項目 ②

- Moving on to the question of the US market, I would say that the prospect is not encouraging.
  接下來是美國市場的問題，我認為前景不是很樂觀。
- Moving on to the issue of dealing with late payers, we need to appeal to their emotions rather than their reason.
  接下來是處理拖欠帳款顧客的問題，我們需要訴諸於他們的感情而不是要求他們講道理。
- Moving on to the earnings in the third quarter, we see that our sales got back on track.
  接下來是第三季的盈餘，我們可以看出銷售已經恢復正常。

get back on track 是「回到軌道上」的意思，這個片語很常用來形容開始達到期望水準。

04 To digress for a moment, let's consider the alternatives.

暫時離一下題，請各位想想有沒有替代方案。

在簡報過程中，有時會出現需要提到與主題無關的話題，或是簡報者覺得有需要補充內容的狀況，下面是幾個很好用的表現方式。

說明暫時離題

- To digress a little bit, let me briefly explain the different processes between branding and advertising.
  稍微離一下題，讓我簡單的解釋品牌行銷與廣告的不同程序。
- If you allow me to digress for a moment, let's talk about all the options we have.
  如果各位讓我離一下題，我想談談我們手上有的選擇。

›› 還有這樣的表現方式

Digressing for a moment, I want to talk about the problems resulting from downsizing our organization.
暫時離一下題，我想談談公司組織縮編引起的問題。

Let's pause for a moment here, and let's be reminded of our company's policy on bad debt.
我們暫停一下，大家應該記得公司對於壞帳的政策。

be reminded of 是「被提醒～」的意思，用 remind（提醒、使想起）這個動詞的被動式來表現。

05 That leads us to understand the slow progress on this project.

這讓我們了解到這個計畫進度緩慢的原因。

這是可以用來 link，也就是，用來連接兩個想法的方式。A leads to B 就是 A 這樣的狀況造成了 B 這樣的結果，是很常用的句型。

連結原因與結果

- That leads us to see why we are so successful at this project.
  這讓我們了解到我們能在這個企劃上如此成功的原因。

- That leads us to realize how we have managed to maintain a greater market share than any of the other companies.
  這讓我們了解到我們的市占率能一直維持比其他公司高的原因。

- That leads us to the problem I raised at the beginning of the presentation.
  這就讓我們想到我在簡報開始時提出的問題。

注意，此句中的 to 為介系詞。

›› 還有這樣的表現方式

Then we come to the issue of training our employees.
接著我們要談談員工訓練的問題。

Let's go back to the problem of hiring skilled workers.

讓我們回到雇用熟手的問題上。

短暫離題之後，用來回歸原本主題的表現方式。

有經驗的員工「熟手」：a skilled worker
實習人員：intern
試用員工：probational employee

說明回到主題

- Let's go back to the issue of minimum wage.
  讓我們回到最低工資的問題上。
- Let's go back to the question of restructuring.
  讓我們回到重整的問題上。
- Let's go back to the issue of increasing sales.
  讓我們回到增加銷售的問題上。

›› 還有這樣的表現方式

Going back to the question of restructuring, I would say that we have no choice.
回到重整的問題上，我認為我們沒有別的選擇。

隨堂測驗 A

請用提示的單字完成句子。

1 讓我們從資訊科技的最新發展開始。
(with / start / let's / the / advances / latest)

→ ______________________________ in information technology.

2 接著讓我們談談辦公室保全系統。
(systems / office / move / security / let's / to / the)

→ ____

3 接下來是節省費用的問題，我想先聽聽崔先生的意見。
(on / saving / costs / of / moving / to / the / issue)

→ ____, I want to ask for Mr. Choi's opinion on this first.

4 暫時離一下題，請各位想想有沒有替代方案。
(for / digress / a / moment / to)

→ ________________________, let's consider the alternatives.

5 這讓我們了解到這個計畫進度緩慢的原因。
(leads / to / understand / that / us)

→ _________________________ the slow progress on this project.

6 讓我們回到雇用熟手的問題上。
(back / go / to / problem / let's / the)

→ ______________________________ of hiring skilled workers.

隨堂測驗 B

請參考中文提示完成簡報內容。

MP3 08

1

我們該如何進行**人力縮減**呢？以下是我們該做的。**第一**，重整企業結構，**第二**，關閉海外沒有利潤的工廠，**最後**，請資深員工選擇提早退休。

How are we going to ①________? Here is what we have to do. ②________, reorganize our business structure. ③________, shut down the overseas factories which aren't making profits. ④_______, ask our senior employees to take an early retirement option.

接著，讓我們**從**如何重整企業結構開始。(……)

Then, let's start ⑤________ how to reorganize our business structure. (...)

接下來讓我們談談為何需要關閉海外沒有利潤的工廠。首先，請注**意看**這張說明了我們海外事業狀況的圖表。(……)

Let's ⑥________ on to discuss why we have to close our unprofitable overseas factories. To begin with, I want you to ⑦________ on the chart which shows how our overseas business is doing. (...)

2

讓我們從最後夢幻 2018 企劃的主要**目標**開始，(……)

① ________ start with the principle ② ________ of the Final Fantasy 2018 project. (...)

接下來讓我們看看這個企劃的任務。那就是……。

Let's ③ ________ on to the mission of this project. Its mission is to ....

如果容許我**離一下題**，讓我**簡短**說明這個遊戲的內容。(……)

If you will allow me to ④ ________ a little, let me ⑤ ________ talk about what the game will be about. (...)

這就是我們計畫要開發的遊戲的大概情形。接著我們**要談談**了解目前市場狀況與攻占市場之策略的問題。(……)

That pretty much covers what we need to know about the game we are planning to make. Then we ⑥ ________ to the issue of understanding the current market situation and our strategy to penetrate it. (...)

現在讓我們**回到**要如何資助這個企劃的問題。

Now, let us go ⑦ ________ to the problem of how we are going to finance this project.

Bonus

有效果的簡報訊息傳達技術

速度與節奏 (Tempo)

運用不同的說話速度。一直使用同一個速度說話的話，聽眾很容易感到無聊，最好偶爾用短暫的沉默來讓聽眾思考。

聲音 (Voice)

調整聲音的聲量與高低，有時高有時低，有時小聲有時大聲，這樣的變化除了能避免聽眾的注意力渙散之外，更能充分地強調內容重點。

句子 (Sentence)

盡量使用簡潔的句子。如果主詞跟敘述詞之間有過多的修飾語，或是使用一堆連接詞讓句子過長的話，效果會很差。

強調與模糊化 (Emphasizers and Minimizers)

適當的運用 extremely, entirely, absolutely, completely 等這些有誇張意味的字詞以及 appear, seems, perhaps, might be, tend to 等這些較為模糊的語彙，會讓簡報訊息的傳達更有效果。

隨堂測驗 A

1 Let's start with the latest advances 2 Let's move to the office security systems.
3 Moving on to the issue of saving costs 4 To digress for a moment
5 That leads us to understand 6 Let's go back to the problem

隨堂測驗 B

1 ① downsize ② First[Firstly] ③ Second[Secondly] ④ Last[Lastly] ⑤ with ⑥ move ⑦ focus
2 ① Let's ② objectives[goals / aims] ③ move ④ digress ⑤ briefly ⑥ come ⑦ back

Week 1 複習時間

A. 使用下面的單字完成句子。

charge	explain	take	digress
between	looked	consider	

1 I am in ___________ of the special project teams at S Motors.
我負責 S 汽車公司的特別企劃小組。

2 I'd like to ___________ the three most important features of our new product.
我想說明一下我們新產品的三大重要特色。

3 My presentation can be ___________ at under the following topics.
我的簡報可以由以下幾個主題來看。

4 My presentation will ___________ about 15 minutes.
我的簡報長約 15 分鐘。

5 Well, ___________ for a moment that you are the boss of this company.
嗯，請想像一下你是這間公司的老闆。

6 To ___________ a little bit, let me briefly explain the different processes ___________ branding and advertising.
稍微離一下題，讓我簡短說明品牌行銷與廣告的不同程序。

B. 使用提示句完成下列句子。

1 感謝各位百忙中抽空前來。

Hint Thank you for -ing

→ ______________________________

2 這個簡報的主題是「如何改善我們的產能」。

Hint the subject of this presentation

→ ______________________________

3 我會從簡單概述我的簡報開始。

Hint begin by -ing / a brief outline

→ ______________________________

4 統計資料顯示，實際薪資每年成長 12%。

Hint Statistics show that ~ / have been + -ing

→ ______________________________

5 各位有過必須自己帶領企劃小組的經驗嗎？

Hint Have you ever been in a situation where ~?

→ ______________________________

6 這就讓我們想到我在簡報開始時提出的問題。

Hint That leads us to ~

→ ______________________________

C. 根據提示完成下面簡報的空格。 MP3 09

1

Good afternoon, everyone. I _______ _______ to this monthly sales meeting. My name is Erin Lin and I am working for the _______ _______. Today I am going to talk about _______ _______ _______ our sales revenues.

The answer lies in how to diversify distribution channels for our products. First, _______ _______ about who our target consumers are.

各位午安，歡迎各位來參加本月的業務會議，我叫林艾琳，在行銷部工作。今天我要跟各位談談如何提高我們的銷售量。
答案就在於如何讓我們產品的銷售管道更為多元化。首先，讓我們想想誰是我們的目標顧客。

2

There are three stages involved. First the background, then the present situation, and finally the prospects for the future. (...)

_______, I'll examine overseas markets. _______, we will take a look at domestic markets. _______, I will outline efficient ways to penetrate markets.

一共涉及三個階段，第一是背景，然後是現況，最後是未來的展望。(……)
首先，我會檢視一下海外市場，接著，我們會看一下國內市場。最後，我會點出進入市場的有效方法。

3

________ you ever ________ in a situation ________ ________ you've had to prepare your own business plan? In this case, there are many things you have to consider, such as your objectives, mission, financial plan, market analysis summary, strategy and implementation summary, risks, and so on.

________ ________ ________, I will ________ ________ some key elements to making a successful business plan.

各位有過必須自己準備事業計畫的經驗嗎？在這種狀況下你需要考慮許多事情，比方像你的目的、任務、財務計畫、市場分析總結、策略與執行總結、風險等等。
在這個簡報中，我會談談一個成功事業計畫所需要的重點要素。

Answers

A 1 charge 2 explain 3 looked 4 take 5 consider 6 digress / between

B 1 Thank you for taking time off from your busy schedule.
2 The subject of this presentation is "how to improve our productivity."
3 I will begin by giving you a brief outline of my talk.
4 Statistics show that real wages have been increasing by 12% per year.
5 Have you ever been in a situation where you had to lead a project team?
6 That leads us to the problem I raised at the beginning of this presentation.

C 1 welcome you / Marketing Department / how to increase / let's think
2 Firstly / Then / Finally
3 Have / been / in which / In this presentation / talk about

Week 2

進行篇①

星期六第一堂課 介紹視覺資料

星期六第二堂課 分析視覺資料 (1)

星期日第一堂課 分析視覺資料 (2)

星期日第二堂課 有效果的簡報說話方式

複習時間

Week

2

介紹視覺資料

Why don't we look at the bar graphs?

》跟著崔副理一起看看介紹與活用視覺資料的過程中必須用到的表達方式。

介紹視覺資料

我要給各位看一些圖表。

I have some charts to show you.

確認清晰度

各位看到了嗎？

Can you see that?

看到這個圖表，我們可以知道～。

Looking at this graph, we see that ~.

Kate 老師的重點提示

- □ **數字 figure** 除了「型態、樣貌」的意思之外也有「數字」的意思，the figure 6 就是 6 這個數字，six figures 則是指六位數的數字，而「用數字來表示～」就是 express ~ numerically。
- □ **看 look at** 這個「看」可以用來抓住對方的注意力，相對的，see 單純就只是用眼睛看。在簡報中要聽眾「看這個柱狀圖」的話，應該說 look at the bar graph。
- □ **注意，集中 focus on** 後面接受詞，也可以替換成 concentrate on。
- □ **表示 represent** 是用來說明資料代表含義的動詞，也可以替換成 illustrate, show, tell 這些單字，比方說 This dotted line represents ~（這條虛線代表～）。
- □ **組織圖 organization chart** 指的是將公司組織圖示化。
- □ **一部分 portion** 是指整體的一部分，意同於 part。
- □ **連續地 in a raw** 指「一排」或是「連續地」的意思，複數 in rows 的話，是指「幾排」的意思。

將注意力引到圖表上

我要請各位注意這個柱狀圖。

I'd like us to focus on this bar graph.

分析資料

透過資料提出見解

不論你如何解釋，這個圖表都說明～。

However you try to explain it, this graph tells ~.

如果各位看這個圖表，就會知道～。

If you take a look at this graph, you will see ~.

各位從這個圖表上可以看出，已有～。

As you can see from the graph, there has been ~.

Key Expressions 6

視覺資料是簡報不可或缺的要素，因為數據化和圖表化的資料比起十句說明的話更能有效傳達簡報內容。接著就一起來熟悉說明視覺資料的表達方式吧！

MP3 10

這是我的
生活計畫表。
大家知道了嗎？

01 Let me illustrate this point with some figures.

讓我用幾個數據來說明這一點。

視覺資料可作為簡報內容的根據，傳達出事實與資訊並幫助聽眾更加了解簡報的內容。提出視覺資料時可以用下面的句型。

提出事先準備的視覺資料

- Let me illustrate this point with a bar graph.
  讓我用柱狀圖來說明這一點。
- Let me illustrate this point with some tables.
  讓我用幾個表來說明這一點。
- Let me illustrate this point with some statistical data.
  讓我用一些統計數據來說明這一點。

除了 illustrate 之外，也可以用 explain 或是 elaborate。

›› 還有這樣的表現方式

I prepared flow charts **to explain** this point in detail.
我準備了流程圖來詳細解釋這一點。

I have some graphs **which will help you to understand** this plan.
我有幾個圖表可以幫助大家了解這個計畫。

I'd like to show you a bar graph, **which shows** the sales figures during the second quarter according to age groups.
我準備了一個柱狀圖，圖中顯示依不同年齡層在第二季的銷售數字。

02 Why don't we look at the bar graphs?

我們何不看看這個柱狀圖？

這也是介紹視覺資料的表現方式。Why don't we ~? 是最常用的勸誘句型之一，可以用動詞句型 take a look at 或是 have a look at 來讓聽衆的視線集中到視覺資料上。

介紹視覺資料

• Why don't we look at the pie chart?
我們何不看看這個圓餅圖？

• Why don't we look at the table?
我們何不看看這個表？

• Why don't we look at the diagrams?
我們何不看看這個圖表？

請熟悉各種視覺資料的名稱。
表 (table)、柱狀圖 (bar graph)、圓餅圖 (pie chart)、流程圖 (flow chart)、圖表 (diagram)
（參考 77,89 頁的 bonus）

›› 還有這樣的表現方式

Let's take a look at the graph, which shows the sales figures of our overseas subsidiaries.
讓我們看看這個圖表，表中顯示了我們海外分公司的業績數字。

03 I'd like us to concentrate on the figure in this box.

我要請各位注意這個格子裡的數字。

介紹完視覺資料之後，可以用以下的句型來將聽眾的視線移到接下來要說明的地方，傳達出這個資料很重要，請大家集中注意的意涵。

讓聽眾注意視覺資料

- I'd like us to concentrate on this solid line.
  我要請各位注意這個實線。
- I'd like us to focus on the profit figures for a minute.
  我要請各位注意一下這個利潤數字。
- I'd like us to look at the consumption of milk in 2016.
  我要請各位注意 2016 年牛奶的消費量。

I'd like 人 to 動詞：我希望（請）～怎樣～。

›› 還有這樣的表現方式

I'd like to draw your attention to this organization chart.
我希望各位注意這個組織圖。

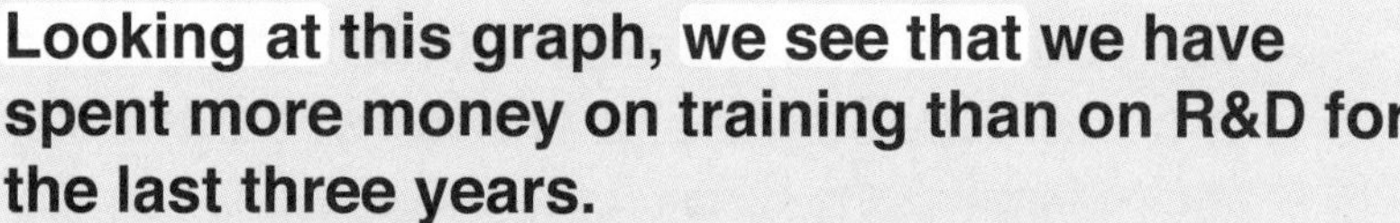

04 Looking at this graph, we see that we have spent more money on training than on R&D for the last three years.

看這個圖表，我們可以知道在過去三年中我們花費在培訓上的資金比研發多。

用現在分詞來介紹圖表的同時加上詳細的說明 (commenting)，這種狀況最適合的主詞是 we。

分析視覺資料 ①

- Looking at the graph more closely, we see that we have gradually expanded our workforce over a ten-year period.
  仔細一點看這個圖表，我們可以知道過去十年來我們的人力漸漸地擴展。
- Looking at this chart carefully, we see that there are some redundant job positions.
  仔細看這張圖表，我們可以看到有些工作職位是多餘的。
- Looking at this diagram, we see how the product is delivered to our customers.
  看這個圖表，我們就可以知道產品是怎樣送到顧客那裡的。

›› 還有這樣的表現方式

If you take a look at this graph, **you will see** there has been a slight increase in the advertising budget.
如果各位看這個圖，就會知道廣告的預算有微幅的增加。

05 As you can see from this chart, there has been a considerable rise in workers' salaries.

各位從這張圖表可以看出，勞工的薪資已有相當大的成長。

可以用 As you can see from ～（各位從～可以看出）來將聽衆的注意力轉移到特定的視覺資料上。若能搭配雷射筆指出該資料的位置，便能更有效地集中聽衆注意力。

分析視覺資料 ②

- As you can see from this graph, the average age of our workforce has been getting younger and younger over the years.
  各位從這張圖可以看出，我們員工的平均年齡近年來愈來愈年輕化。
- As you can see from this pie chart, our profit margin takes up a very small portion.
  各位從這個圓餅圖可以看出，我們的利潤只占了非常小的一部分。
- As you can see from this table, the changes in the weather patterns are due to the greenhouse effect.
  各位從這個表格可以看出，天氣型態的變化是因為溫室效應所引起的。

請注意不及物動詞 rise 和及物動詞 raise 的差別。
- Black, dense smoke rose up.（濃厚的黑煙升起。）
- They raised the flag as a sign of surrender.（他們升起白旗表示投降。）

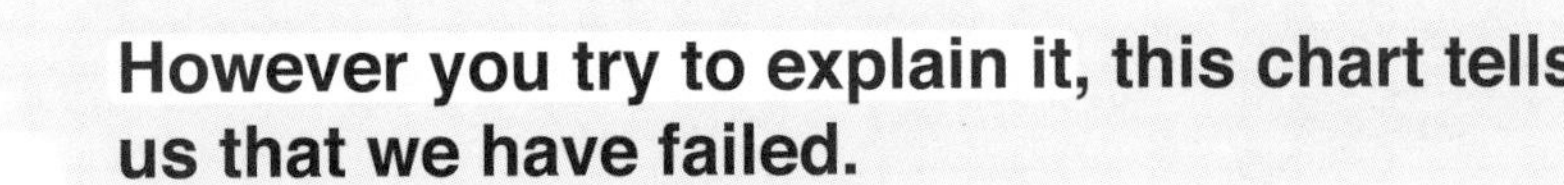

However you try to explain it, this chart tells us that we have failed.

不管你如何解釋，這個圖表都說明我們失敗了。

視覺資料的使用目的很多，當簡報者想要用視覺資料堅持自己的主張時，可以用以下這種表達方式。

帶出簡報者的主張

- However you try to explain it, this chart demonstrates that we will fail unless we keep our prices low.
  不管你如何解釋，這張圖表都顯示我們會失敗，除非我們維持低價。
- However you try to explain it, the fact is that our sales have gone down over the years.
  不管你如何解釋，事實就是過去幾年我們的業績已經下滑了。
- However you try to explain it, the graph shows that our production has flattened for three years in a row.
  不管你如何解釋，圖表顯示我們的生產連續三年都沒有成長。

›› 還有這樣的表現方式

Whatever the reason for this, it can't account for our low productivity.
不管原因為何，都不能解釋我們產能的低落。

Whichever way you look at it, the fact is that our turnover has not risen.
不管各位怎麼看，事實就是我們的營業額沒有提升。

隨堂測驗 A

請用提示的單字完成句子。

1 我們何不看看這個柱狀圖？
(at / not / do / we / why / look)

→ ______________________________ the bar graphs?

2 讓我用柱狀圖來說明這一點。
(me / this / point / illustrate / let / with)

→ ____________________________________ a bar graph.

3 我要請各位注意一下這個利潤數字。
(concentrate / like / to / on / I'd / us)

→ __________________________________ the profit figures for a minute.

4 看到這個圖表，我們可以知道過去三年中我們花費在培訓上的資金比研發多。
(this / see / looking / graph / at / we)

→ ___________________________________ that we have spent more money on training than on R&D.

5 各位從這張圖表可以看出，勞工的薪資已有相當大的成長。
(from / as / see / chart / this / you / can)

→ ____, there has been a considerable rise in workers' salaries.

6 不管你如何解釋，這個圖表都說明我們失敗了。
(explain / you / it / however / to / try)

→ ___________________________________, this chart tells us that we have failed.

隨堂測驗 B

請參考中文提示完成簡報內容。

請各位**注意**這張朝鮮半島的地圖，這裡是「天安」，意思就是天下最平安的地方。

I'd like to draw ①________ ________ to this map of the Korean peninsula. Here you see Cheonan, which means the most comfortable place ②________ heaven.

不過現在我想稱它為韓國交通最方便的地方。**各位從**地圖上**可以看到**，它位於一個交叉點上，離首爾只有 50 分鐘，離大田只有 50 分鐘，離平澤港也只有 20 分鐘。(……)

But now I would call it the most convenient place in Korea in terms of its transportation. ③________ ________ ________ ________ from the map, it stands at a crossroads which will lead you to Seoul in 50 minutes, to Daejeon in 50 minutes, and Pyungtaek Harbor in 20 minutes. (…)

如果各位**看一下**這個圖表**的話**，就可以知道韓國有將近 10% 的大學聚集在這裡。**不管原因為何**，這個數據表示這個區域絕對不缺受過教育的勞工。

If you ④________ ________ ________ at this chart, you will see that almost 10% of Korean universities are packed here in Korea. ⑤________ ________ ________ for this, the figure means that there will be no shortage of educated workers here in this area.

最後，我搜集了一些數據放到這個表裡。從這個表上可以看出，和其他的地方政府相比，天安有多麼想要幫助海外的投資者。

Finally, I have gathered some statistics and put them onto this table. ⑥________ at this table, you will see how much Cheonan desires to help foreign investors compared with other local governments.

這個格子裡的數據**代表**近幾年天安市議會通過的政策。這些各式各樣的**政策**能幫助各位在忠清南道的這個地區建造各位的工廠。

The figure in this box ⑦________ the number of policies the Cheonan city council has passed in recent years. These various ⑧________ will help you to build your factory here in this region of Chungnam Province.

我們可以做出的**結論**非常的明顯，答案就在這裡。

The ⑨________ to be drawn from this are very clear to you. The answer is here.

隨堂測驗 A

1 Why don't we look at 2 Let me illustrate this point with 3 I'd like us to concentrate on
4 Looking at this graph, we see 5 As you can see from this chart
6 However you try to explain it

隨堂測驗 B

① your attention ② under ③ As you can see ④ take a look ⑤ Whatever the reason
⑥ Looking ⑦ represents ⑧ policies ⑨ conclusions

多樣化的視覺資料 (1)

● 柱狀圖 (Bar Graph)

柱狀圖是用長條狀圖形的高度或長度來顯示數量，所以想要比較數量時，經常會用柱狀圖來表示。

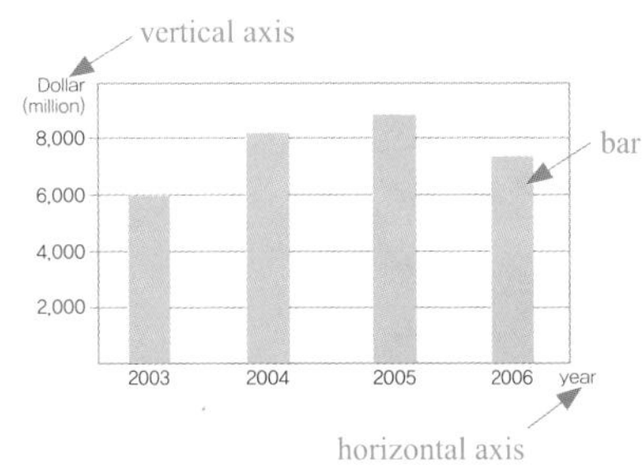

例 **On the vertical axis**, you see the amount of investment we have made, while **on the horizontal axis**, we see the year in which we invested the money.

垂直軸表示我們所做的投資金額，水平軸則表示投資該金額的年度。

● 線條圖 (Line Graph)

通常線條圖的水平軸會標示時間，垂直軸則標示數量，將資料依順序點上之後連成線。

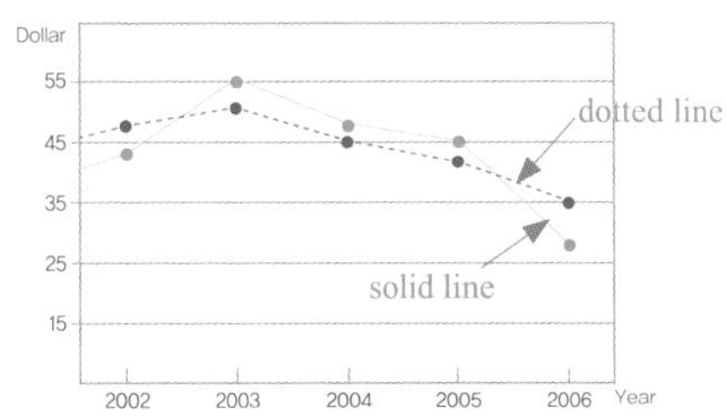

例 **The dotted line** represents profits while **the solid line** stands for total costs.

虛線表示利潤，實線則表示總成本。

● 圓餅圖 (Pie Chart)

這是一種將所有資料放入一個圓餅的圖表。表中每一個扇形表示各類別所占的比率。

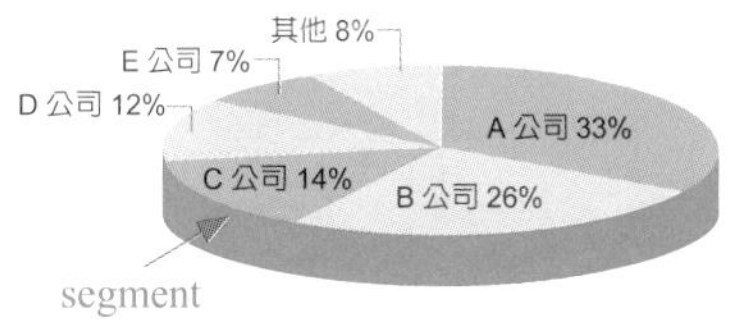

例 In this pie chart we have the total consumption of milk, with each segment representing the top five brands in Taiwan.

這個圓餅圖表示所有牛奶的消費量，而各個區塊則代表台灣的前五大品牌。

Week

2 分析視覺資料 (1)

Productivity has decreased by 10%.

| 星期六第二堂課 |

》跟著崔副理一起看看如何說明數量的變化。

增加

我們的產量增加了。

- Our production has increased.
- Our production has been on the rise.

急速增加

公司的利潤急速成長 30%。

The company's profits shot up by 30%.

微幅的增減

～有微幅的增加〔減少〕。

There has been a slight increase[decrease] in ~.

減少

利潤減少了。

- Profitability has decreased.
- Profitability has been on the decline.

急速滑落

股價急速下跌。

Shares have slumped.

Kate 老師的重點提示

- □ **增加** increase 要說明從過去到現在一定的時間內數據有增加時，須用現在完成式 have / has increased 來表示。此外，rise 和 grow 也是表示增加的動詞。
- □ **減少** decrease 除了用 decrease 來表示銷售量跟利潤等的數據下降之外，也可以用 fall 或是 go down。
- □ **若干，些微的** slight 表示微小的量或是程度，a slight decrease（些微的減少）也可以用 a bit、a little 來替換。
- □ **穩定地** steadily 可以用 steadily / constantly /continuously 這些副詞來說明穩定的增加或減少。
- □ **波動，變化** fluctuate 當現象不穩定或有大變化的時候可以用 fluctuate 來表現。
- □ **相當的** substantial 表示量跟大小等「相當的多」，與 considerable 一樣意思。
- □ **恢復，回到原本的狀態** recover 後面可接介系詞 from 來表示「從～恢復過來」，例如 recover from the economic hardships 意即「從經濟蕭條恢復過來」。
- □ **維持狀態，持續** maintain

穩定的狀態

銷量穩定。

Sales have remained steady.

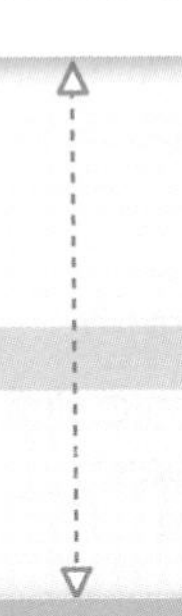

不穩定的狀態

台灣加權股價指數一直有波動。

The TAIEX has been fluctuating.

恢復的狀態

我們的銷量已經完全恢復了。

Our sales have completely recovered.

Key Expressions 6

如果想要有效果的將視覺資料中的情報傳達給聽衆，就要先分析視覺資料，正確地表現出增減變化等趨勢。下面是幾種用來呈現視覺資料中數量變化的方式。

MP3 12

01 Our sales have steadily increased over the years.

我們的銷量幾年來一直有穩定的增加。

分析視覺資料時必須用到幾種說明方法。首先是說明「增加」的方法。動詞除了 increase 之外，也可以用 rise / go up / grow / expand 等。

增加，向上

- Interest rates have considerably increased.
  利息有相當程度的增加。
- Our profits have gone up during the summer.
  我們的利潤夏季時有成長。
- Our production has grown for the first time since the IMF period.
  自 IMF 期間以來我們的生產量第一次有了成長。
- Our export figures have expanded gradually.
  我們的出口數量有逐漸地成長。

>> 還有這樣的表現方式

In the fourth quarter, the company's profits **shot up** by 30%.
公司的利潤在第四季急速成長了 30%。

Productivity has decreased by 10%.

產能減少了 10%。

分析視覺資料所代表的意義時，除了增長之外，當然也可能要說明減少的狀況，此時動詞除了用 decrease 之外，也可以用 fell / decline / go down / shrink 等。

減少，萎縮

- Profitability has fallen rapidly.
  利潤急速減少。
- The domestic market has shrunk significantly.
  國內市場有顯著的萎縮。
- The bank's net profits plunged 71% last year.
  去年銀行的淨利銳減了 71%。
- Sales have declined for the last two months.
  過去兩個月的銷售量減少了。
- Our productivity has gone down this summer.
  今年夏季我們的產能減少了。

›› 還有這樣的表現方式

Shares **have slumped** from $25 to $12.
股價從 25 美金大跌到 12 美金。

Chicken stocks **have lost** roughly 100 points since the outbreak of bird flu.
雞肉相關股票從禽流感爆發以來已經跌了大約 100 點。

slump: 大跌，突然衰退
lose: 遭受損失，價值、效力等減少

03 There has been a slight increase in worker's salaries.

勞工的薪資有微幅的增加。

在說明「變化」和「發展」的狀態時有許多表達方式，讓我們先來看看特別與「增加」及「減少」相關的用法。

微幅的增加或減少

- There has been a slight gain in our market share.

  我們的市占率有微幅的成長。

- There has been a slight decrease in our GDP by 0.01%.

  我們的國內生產總值微幅的減少了 0.01%。

- There has been a slight fall of sales figures.

  銷售量有微幅的下滑。

句中 slight 的部分可以用 rapid 或是 unexpected 等各樣的形容詞來說明資料的內容。

>> 還有這樣的表現方式

There has been **rapid growth** in the advertising industry.
廣告產業有急速的成長。

We have witnessed **an unexpected dip** in the stock market.
我們見到股市無預警地下跌。

There was **a dramatic increase** in heating-oil consumption last winter due to record-breaking, cold temperatures.
去年冬天由於破紀錄的低氣溫，使得暖氣燃油的消耗量急遽的增加。

The government move will stabilize property prices.

政府的措施將會穩定不動產的價格。

說明價格或是銷量在高低起伏後「穩定地」停在一定水準時，可用 stabilize 這個字，其名詞型是 stabilization，形容詞型是 steady。

這裡的 move 是指政府的「動作」，也就是「措施」；property 則是「不動產、財產」的意思。

穩定

- Exchange rates will soon be stabilized.
  匯率很快就會穩定下來。
- Everybody wants the stabilization of oil prices.
  大家都希望油價穩定。
- The IMF relief fund will have a stabilizing effect on the economy.
  國際貨幣基金組織的救濟基金對經濟會有穩定的效果。

›› 還有這樣的表現方式

Sales **have remained steady**.
銷售量維持穩定。

We must **maintain the status quo** for the time being.
目前我們必須維持現狀。

maintain the status quo: 維持現狀

05 Our sales have recovered completely.

我們的銷售額已經完全恢復。

要說明景氣在經過一段時間的低落之後「恢復」的情形可用 recover。另外，原意為「撿起～」的 pick up，也可以用來形容「恢復」。

恢復

- The stock market index has gradually begun to recover.
  股市指數已逐漸開始回升。
- Interest rate cuts have failed to bring about economic recovery in our country.
  在我國，利率的降低並沒有帶來經濟的復甦。
- In many sectors of the economy, the recovery has started.
  經濟的許多方面都已經開始復甦。

›› 還有這樣的表現方式

Our export sales have slowly **picked up**.
我們的出口銷量已慢慢地回升。

The stock market will **improve** by summer.
股票市場到夏季就會好轉。

除此之外，也可以用動詞 rally 來表示恢復穩定或回升。

06 The TAIEX has been fluctuating between 9,600 and 9,700.

台灣加權股價指數在 9,600 跟 9,700 之間波動。

政策、物價、意見、想法、天氣等等不斷地在變化、波動時，可以用 fluctuate / the ups and downs / roller-coaster 等來表達。

波動

- It is difficult to fix the price because of the constantly fluctuating price of crude oil.
  由於原油價格不斷地波動，價格很難固定下來。

- The fluctuation in the price should be taken into consideration.
  價格的波動應該要列入考量。

- Stock prices fluctuate throughout the day.
  股價整天不斷地波動。

›› 還有這樣的表現方式

The Dow Jones index shows **the ups and downs** of the market during the war period.
在戰爭期間，道瓊指數顯示嚴重的波動。

Over the last few years, we have seen the popularity of our products **take a roller-coaster ride**.
過去幾年來，我們見到我們產品人氣的大幅起落。

隨堂測驗 A

請用提示的單字完成句子。

1 我們的銷量幾年來一直有穩定的增加。
(have / over / increased / the / years / steadily)

→ Our sales ________________________.

2 國內市場有顯著的萎縮。
(significantly / shrunk / has)

→ The domestic market ________________________.

3 勞工的薪資有微幅的增加。
(there / a / been / has / increase / slight)

→ ________________________ in worker's salaries.

4 匯率很快就會穩定下來。
(be / soon / will / stabilized)

→ Exchange rates ________________________.

5 我們的銷售額已經完全恢復。
(sales / completely / our / recovered / have)

→ ________________________.

6 台灣加權股價指數在 9,600 跟 9,700 之間波動。
(9,700 / between / fluctuating / 9,600 / and / been / has)

→ The TAIEX ________________________.

隨堂測驗 B

請參考中文提示完成簡報內容。

我準備了一些**視覺資料**可以讓各位清楚地了解我們海外市場目前的狀況。

I have prepared some ①________ which will clearly show you what is going on in our overseas markets.

首先從亞洲市場開始。正如各位從這個圖表**可以看到**，整體的營業額**逐漸下滑**。五年前的數字約為一百五十萬美金，但是現在大概是在一百到一百二十萬美金之間。

Let's start with the Asian markets. As ②________ ________ ________ on this graph, the overall turnover has been ③________ ________. Five years ago, it stood at 1.5 million dollars. But now it's at somewhere between 1 million and 1.2 million dollars.

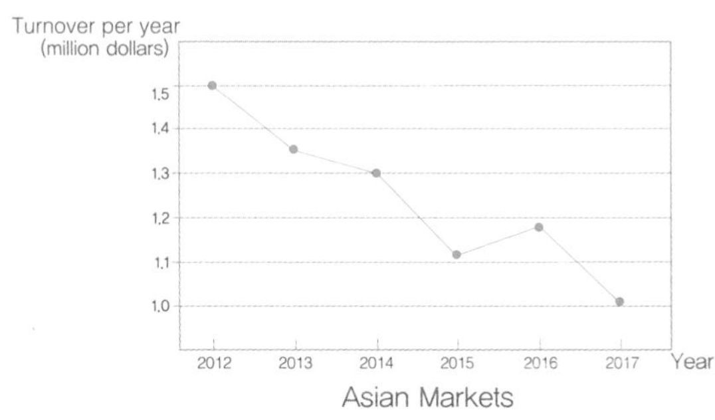

還好的是，美國分公司的數字**稍微好一點**。

Fortunately, however, the figures for our U.S. subsidiary are ④________ ________.

請看這張圖表。各位可以發現從五年前我們開業以來，整體的營業額就**有穩定的增加**。在過去五年間，美國市場持續有穩定的**成長**，現在我們的營業額已經達到兩百萬美金左右。

Please take a look at this graph. You see our turnover has been ⑤________ ________ since we started our business five years ago. During these five years, the U.S. market has continued to ⑥________ steadily, and our turnover now is around 2 million dollars.

這些數據代表的意義很簡單。除非我們想辦法修正亞洲市場的問題，要不然我們在那裡肯定會繼續的**賠錢**。

What these figures suggest is simple. Unless we do something to fix the problems in the Asian markets, we anticipate that we will continue to ⑦________ money there.

隨堂測驗 A

1 have steadily increased over the years 2 has shrunk significantly
3 There has been a slight increase 4 will soon be stabilized
5 Our sales have recovered completely 6 has been fluctuating between 9,600 and 9,700

隨堂測驗 B

① visuals ② you can see ③ gradually declining[decreasing] ④ slightly better
⑤ steadily rising[increasing] ⑥ grow ⑦ lose

多樣化的視覺資料 (2)

● 一覽表 (Table)

為了讓人一眼就看清楚，將數字或文字等情報有組織的放入列 (row) 與行 (column) 組成的表格內。

地區	1999	2000	2001	2002
北美	23,210	23,473	23,441	23,487
中南美	4,705	4,662	4,684	4,590
歐洲	19,630	19,410	19,539	19,406
歐亞大陸	4,304	4,320	4,309	4,338
中東	2,439	2,451	2,481	2,527

row
column
cell

例 **In the rows** we have the yearly consumption of oil energy per capita for each country. **In the columns** we have the different years.
每一列是各國人均年石油消費量，每一行則是各年度數據。

● 流程圖 (Flow Chart)

在平面圖或是立體圖上，將作業流程或路徑用線連起來標示的一種圖表。

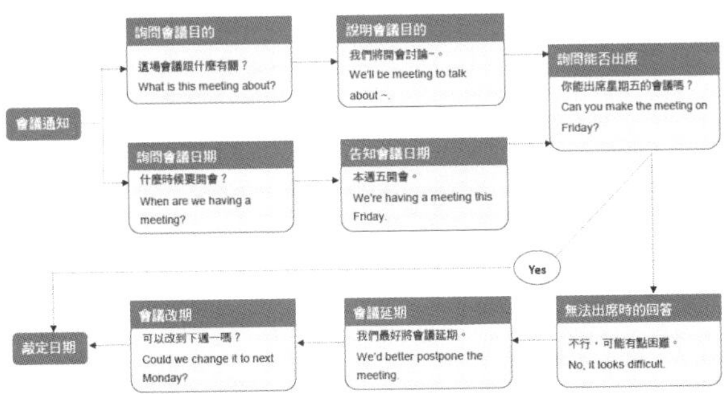

例 **The upper half of the chart** shows the process of setting up a meeting. And **the lower half of the chart** shows the process of arranging a date for a meeting.
圖表上半部顯示了召開會議的流程，下半部則是訂定會議日期的流程。

Week

2

| 星期日第一堂課 |

分析視覺資料 (2)

The turnover is below our expectations.

〉〉跟著崔副理一起看看表現數量程度與狀態的方法吧！

期望以上

利潤超過我們的預期。

The profitability is over our expectations.

達到最高

我們的利潤率在上個月達到最高點。

Our profitability reached its peak last month.

大略／附近

～費用落在大約 500 美金到 600 美金之間。

~ costs fall somewhere between 500 and 600 dollars.

期望以下

營業額不如我們的預期。

The turnover is below our expectations.

到達最低

通貨膨脹率在上個月觸底。

Inflation rates bottomed out last month.

- □ **大約、略估** approximately 表示數據並不精確、只是大略的，與 roughly 同義。
- □ **頂峰、最高點** peak 名詞，用來形容「最頂尖處」，例如 reach one's peak 意即「達到某種最高」紀錄。
- □ **約～，在～附近** in the region of 後面加上數字時，就是「約～」的意思。
- □ **不到～，未達～** short of 貨物量或是數字不到某個基準點時，可以用 A is short of B 來表示，或是 A is below B。
- □ **超過** exceed 這個動詞是表示數量超過某個基準點，也可以用 be over，如 A is over B 即表達同樣意思。
- □ **比～多** more than 相反的「比～少」就是 less than。
- □ **銷售利潤** margin 總銷售金額減去成本和銷售費用，也就是銷售得到的利潤。另外，「純益」則是 net profit。
- □ **收入與支出打平** break-even「損益平衡點」就是 break-even point。

超過

有機食品的需求超過了供給。

The demand for organic foods exceeds the supply.

不足

我們的營業額差一點就達到兩百萬美金。

Our turnover is just short of 2 million dollars.

Key Expressions 6

接下來要說明在簡報分析視覺資料中，當數值比一定基準點高或低時的表現方式，以及達到最高點、最低點和接近某個基準點時的表現方式。

您好，
久仰大名。
喂！相親是在那一桌啦！
沒睡醒是吧！

01 Equipment costs are over 100,000 dollars.

設備成本超過十萬美金。

這是表達「比～高，超過～」的說法，over 就是 more than 的意思。

說明「超過～（～以上）」的狀況

- Profitability is well over our expectations.
  利潤遠超過我們的預期。
- Expenditures on education are well over our expectations.
  教育上的支出遠超過我們的預期。
- The economic growth rates are just over the government's predictions.
  經濟成長率剛好超過政府的預測。
- This year's budget is slightly over our original projection because of additional expenditures on the purchase of new equipment.
  由於購買新設備的額外支出，今年度的預算略高於我們原本的預期。

02 Our profitability reached its peak last month.

我們的利潤率在上個月達到頂點。

要形容獲利或是銷售量「達到」某個基準點時，可使用有「抵達」某個頂點意味的動詞 reach。reach one's peak 是指「達到最高點」，而要說明「達到最低點」則可用 bottom out。

說明「達到頂點／落底」的狀況

- Our productivity reached its peak last year.
  我們的產能在去年達到最高點。
- Inflation rates bottomed out last month.
  通貨膨脹率在上個月觸底。
- The price of oil reached a new high last week.
  油價在上週漲到了新高。

›› 還有這樣的表現方式

Unemployment **peaked at** 6.2%.
失業率達到 6.2% 的最高紀錄。

Housing prices **bottomed out**.
房價觸底了。

We expect sales figures in health food to **bottom out**.
我們預期健康食品的銷售數字將會觸底。

peak 和 bottom 這兩個動詞本身就有「達到頂峰／觸底」的意思。

03 The turnover is below our expectations.

營業額低於我們的預期。

「比～低」通常是用 be below 來表現，為了不混淆 below 跟 under，讓我們確實比較一下兩者的差異。be under 是「在某物下方」的意思（也包含被某物覆蓋著），也就是 being directly lower(直接在下方)。below 則是「與某物有距離，比其物低」的意思，也就是 being on a lower level（在較低的位置）。

說明「沒有達到／未達～」的狀況

- Their price is well below our expectations.
  他們的價格遠低於我們的預期。
- Expenditure this year should be just below 1.5 million dollars.
  今年度的支出應該剛好比一百五十萬美金低一些。
- Our sales revenue is below our expectations.
  我們的營業收入比預期低。
- We have to keep overall price increases 4.5% below inflation.
  我們必須把總價格上揚率維持在低於通貨膨脹率 4.5%。
- This year, productivity has been below average.
  今年度的生產力低於平均水平。

04 Our total costs for this month are expected to be somewhere between 50,000 and 60,000 dollars.

我們這個月的總成本預計大約會在五到六萬美金之間。

Somewhere between A and B 是用於說明某個大略數據的區間。

說明「在～之間」的狀況

- The CEO is believed to earn somewhere between 1 million and 1.2 million dollars per year.
  執行長每年的收入被認為大約在一百到一百二十萬美金之間。
- Our operating costs per month fall somewhere between 2 million and 3 million NT.
  我們每個月的營運成本大約在兩百到三百萬台幣之間。
- Our turnover stays somewhere between 3.5 and 4 million dollars.
  我們的營業額大約維持在三百五十到四百萬美金之間。

›› 還有這樣的表現方式

The project will cost **in the region of** 10 million dollars.
這個計畫的成本將會是一千萬美金左右。

05 Our turnover is just short of two million dollars.

我們的營業額差一點就達到兩百萬美金。

be short of 是「不到某個數量」的意思，跟 less than 同義。

說明「不足～」的狀況

- We are still one million dollars short of our target.
  我們距離目標還差一百萬美金。
- This investment has left our company short of money.
  這項投資使得我們公司資金短缺。
- The company fell short of its sales goal last month.
  該公司上個月沒有達到銷售目標。

›› 還有這樣的表現方式

The targeted gross margin for the first year is **a little less than** 2 million dollars.
第一年的目標毛利比兩百萬美金低一些。

The sudden increase in population has resulted in **a shortage of** housing.
人口的突然增加造成了住屋的不足。

Production levels in Vietnam exceed the rest.

越南的生產水平超過其他國家。

exceed 是用來表達數量或是比率、規模「超過」某個特定點，也可以用 be more than 或是 be greater than 來替換。

表達「超過」時

- Our R&D budget exceeds 1 million dollars a year.
  我們的研發費用每年超過一百萬美金。
- The demand for organic foods exceeds the supply.
  有機食品的需求超過供給。
- Our performance has exceeded all expectations.
  我們的表現超乎所有人的預期。

›› 還有這樣的表現方式

These findings are based on the survey of **more than** 1,500 customers.
這些發現以針對 1,500 多位顧客所做的調查為基礎。

This survey shows that we can sell our products for **more than** 10 dollars each.
這個調查讓我們知道我們可以把產品賣到每個十塊美金以上。

隨堂測驗 A

請用提示的單字完成句子。

1 利潤遠超過我們的預期。
(our / over / well / expectations / is)

→ Profitability ______________________________.

2 我們的產能在去年達到最高點。
(its / reached / peak / year / last)

→ Our productivity ______________________________.

3 營業額低於我們的預期。
(is / below / expectations / our)

→ The turnover ______________________________.

4 我們每個月的營運成本大約在兩百到三百萬台幣之間。
(costs / fall / somewhere / operating / our / per / month)

→ ______________________________ between 2 million and 3 million NT.

5 我們的營業額差一點就達到兩百萬美金。
(is / of / million / just / two / dollars / short)

→ Our turnover ______________________________.

6 越南的生產水平超過其他國家。
(production / the / rest / in / levels / exceed / Vietnam)

→ ______________________________.

隨堂測驗 B

請參考中文提示完成簡報內容。

1 MP3 15

我們的初創成本達 503,750 美金，**遠高於**原本的計畫，這是因為我們立意要成為 MP3 播放器市場的霸主。

Our start-up costs come to \$503,750, which are ①________ ________ our original plan because of our commitment to dominate the MP3-player market.

只要營業額能達到**大約** 325,000 **到** 350,000 美金**之間**，我們就可以將損益打平。這樣的預測銷售目標是基於市場對線上音樂的需求不斷增加。

We can break even with a sales level of ②________ ________ \$325,000 ③________ \$350,000 per month. The sales forecast is based upon an increasing demand for online music.

我們預計銷量會從 2015 年的五十萬美金升高**到** 2017 年的兩百萬美金。在確保長遠鞏固市場地位的同時，我們預計**至少**會賠錢兩年。

Sales are projected to rise from \$500,000 in 2015 ④________ \$2 million in 2017. We plan to lose money for ⑤________ ________ two years while we secure our long-term position for the future.

2

營業額從 2004 年的兩百萬美金增加到 2005 年的三百萬美金，**超過了**我們的預期。我們希望 2006 年的預計銷售收入可以**達到最高點**。

Sales have increased from $2.0 million in 2004 to $3.0 million in 2005, which has ① ________ our expectations. We hope that the projected sales revenue will ② ________ ________ ________ in 2006.

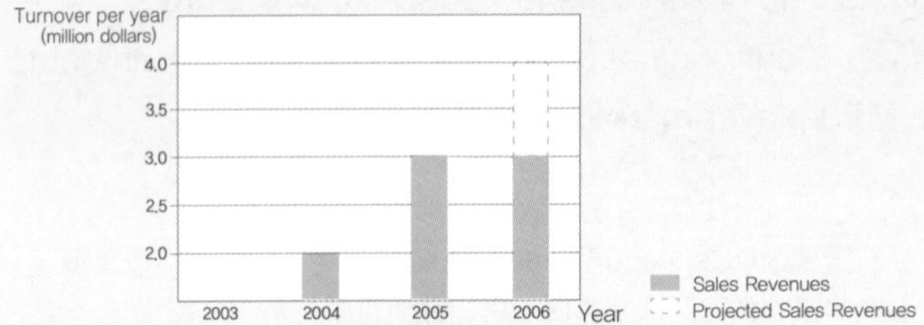

我們的毛利率也增加了 50%，淨利潤率更是超過了 10.75%。我們將會維持至少 30% 的市占率，比原本的預期**低了** 5%。

Our gross margin has also increased to 50% and our net profit margin to more than 10.75%. We will maintain at least a 30% market share, which is 5% ③ ________ ________ our original projection.

隨堂測驗 A

1 is well over our expectations 2 reached its peak last year 3 is below our expectations
4 Our operating costs per month fall somewhere 5 is just short of two million dollars
6 Production levels in Vietnam exceed the rest

隨堂測驗 B

1 ① well over ② somewhere between ③ and ④ to ⑤ at least
2 ① exceeded ② reach its peak ③ short of

數字讀法

分析視覺資料或提供某種數據情報時，數字一定要說對。請記住下列數字的讀法。

1. 數字讀法

讀數字的基本原則是以三個位數為單位，但某些時候也會有兩個位數就斷掉的讀法。

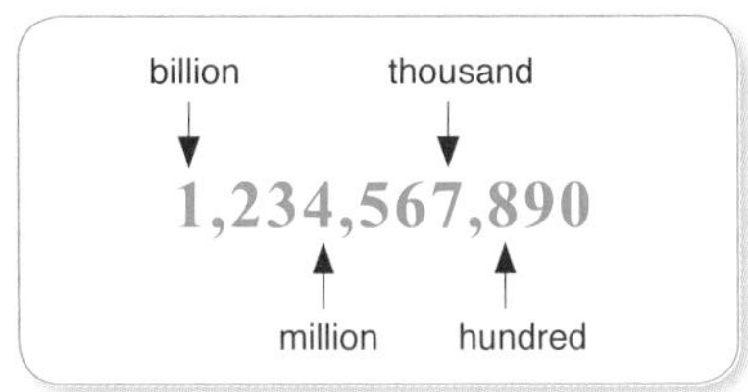

- 436,287,591 : four hundred and thirty-six million, two hundred and eighty-seven thousand, five hundred and ninety-one
- 6,789 : six thousand, seven hundred and eighty-nine
- 1,800 : one thousand eight hundred 或是 eighteen hundred

2. 分數讀法

分子為基數，分母是序數

- 1/2: a[one] half
- 2/3: two thirds
- 3/5: three fifths
- 1/4: one fourth / a quarter
- 1 3/4: one and three quarters

3. 小數點讀法

「點」就是 point，小數點後面的數字要單獨念

- 46.28 : forty-six point two eight
- 0.45 : (zero) point four five
- 5.03 : five point o three

4. 倍數讀法

- 一半：half ／兩倍：double ／三倍：triple ／四倍：quadruple

5. 次數讀法

- 一次：once ／兩次：twice ／三次：three times ／四次：four times

Week

2

有效果的簡報說話方式

The procedure is generally easy to follow.

| 星期日第二堂課 |

〉〉跟著崔副理一起看看如何有邏輯地陳述事實或意見吧！

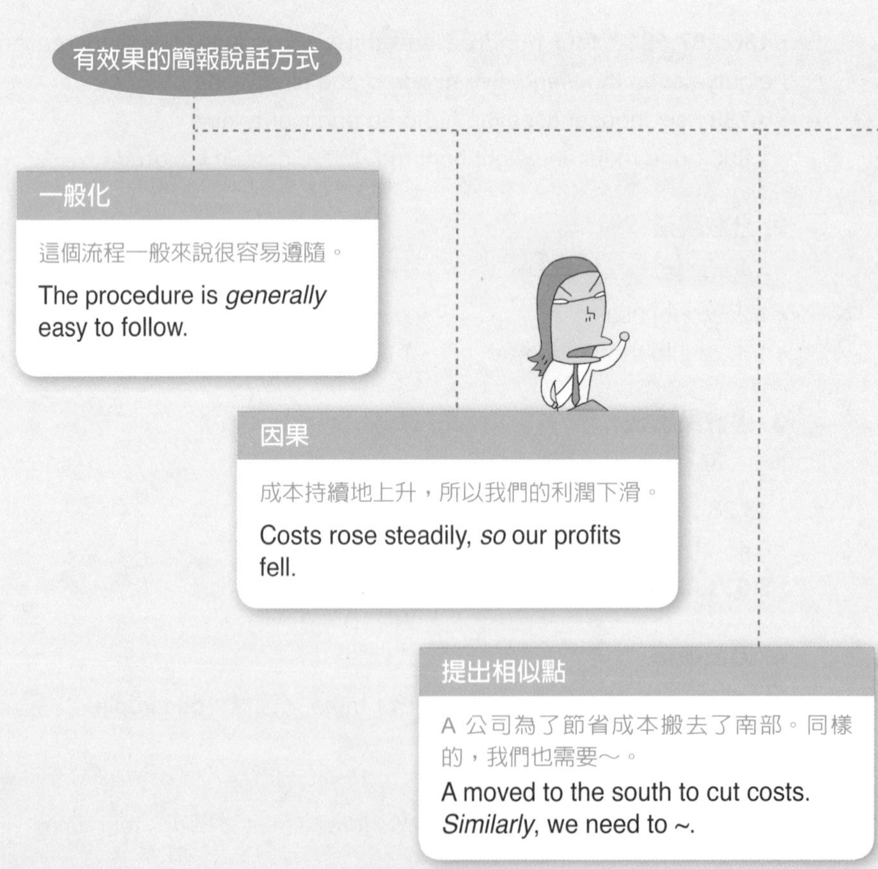

有效果的簡報說話方式
一般化
這個流程一般來說很容易遵隨。
The procedure is *generally* easy to follow.
因果
成本持續地上升，所以我們的利潤下滑。
Costs rose steadily, *so* our profits fell.
提出相似點
A 公司為了節省成本搬去了南部。同樣的，我們也需要～。
A moved to the south to cut costs. *Similarly*, we need to ~.

Kate 老師的重點提示

□ **所以 so** 用於接續原因與結果句（主詞＋動詞）的連接詞，與連接副詞 therefore 同義。

□ **但是 but** 用於接續相反意思句子的連接詞，也可以用連接副詞 however 來表達。

□ **一般來說 generally** 這個副詞用來形容「雖然並非一定，但是大範圍來說都適用的事實與事件」。

□ **多虧了～，由於～ thanks to** 在 to 之後接「事物」。

□ **一點～都沒有 whatsoever** 比 whatever 更加強調，主要用於否定的名詞之後，例如 nothing whatsoever「什麼都沒有」。

□ **其他等等 and so on** and so forth 也表達同樣的意思，口語中不太會用 etc.(et cetera)。

□ **同樣地 similarly** 這個副詞是用來表示後面出現的事實與狀況跟前面提過的事實與狀況相似，likewise 和 in the same way 也有同樣的意思。

對比

大家都說那是不可能的，但是我們還是做到了。

Everybody said that it was impossible, *but* we made it anyway.

逆轉

我們想相信我們仍然首屈一指。而事實上，我們差得太遠了。

We want to believe that we're still number one. *In fact*, we're nowhere.

舉例

在開展～有幾件事必須考慮，比方說，店面的位置。

There're some things to consider in launching ~, *for example*, the location of the shop.

Key Expressions 6

簡報的目的之一就是要「說服聽眾」。接著就來看看如何用因果、對比、相反、比較等敘述方式，有說服力地陳述自己的主張與意見。

MP3 16

01 We always try to listen to our customers, so we could develop a product which satisfies them.

我們總是試著傾聽顧客的聲音，所以才能開發出滿足他們的產品。

以下是在簡報時，用以說明原因 (reasons) 與其導致之結果 (results) 的表達方式。

說明結果或理由

- Costs rose steadily for the fifth year running, so our profits fell.
  費用五年來持續的上升，所以我們的利潤下滑。
- There have been continuous efforts to improve our services over the last few years, so our customers' satisfaction has increased.
  過去幾年，我們持續努力改善我們的服務，所以顧客的滿意度已有上升。

除了 so 之外，也可以用 as a result 或是 that's why。

» 還有這樣的表現方式

Sales are up **thanks to** our spending more on advertising.
由於我們增加了廣告支出使得銷售量提升。

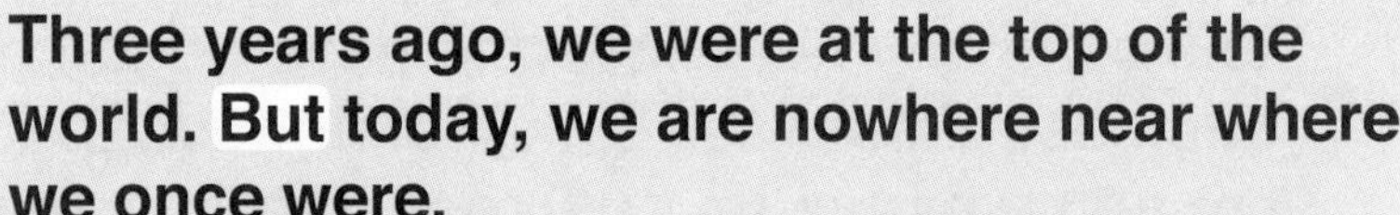

Three years ago, we were at the top of the world. But today, we are nowhere near where we once were.

三年前，我們是世界的領導者。但是今天，我們與過去的地位差得太遠了。

將彼此相反的兩件事放在一起比較的方式稱為「對照法」(contrasting)。上面的句子就是將三年前與現今的狀況放在一起做對比，這樣的句子主要是要強調「但是(but)」後面的內容。

做對比

- Remember it can take years to build a good reputation, but it only takes seconds to lose it.
  要記得，建立良好的信譽可能需要花上多年的時間，但是失去它只需要幾秒鐘。
- Everybody said that it was impossible, but we made it anyway.
  每個人都說那是不可能的，但是我們還是做到了。

> make it 就是「成功的達成某事」的意思。
> 【例】We made it to America after all.（我們成功抵達美國。）
> I believe we have the ability to make it.（我相信我們有能力做到。）

›› 還有這樣的表現方式

The competition in the cosmetics market was very fierce last year. Our sales revenue, **however**, has increased due to our sophisticated designs and low prices.

去年化妝品市場的競爭非常激烈。然而，由於成熟的設計與低價，我們的營業收入有所成長。

We implemented many regulations to keep our costs down last year. **On the contrary**, our costs have gone up slightly because workers were not used to these new regulations.

去年我們為了維持低成本實施了許多規定。相反地，我們的成本卻因為員工們不習慣這些新規定而略為增加。

03 The company is believed to have begun its business before the Gulf War. In fact, the company began its business after the war.

一般以為該公司是在波灣戰爭之前就開始營運。而事實上，是戰爭之後才開始的。

上面的句子用了反駁 (contradiction) 的語法，這種語法是先說出被誤解的點，然後說出事實並非如此，再提出新的事實。

提出相反的事實

- People said that there was no chance for us whatsoever. In fact, there is still a chance for us.
  人們說我們已經再也沒有機會了。而事實上，我們還是有的。

- Everybody in our company wants to believe that we are still the number-one player in the market. In fact, we are nowhere near that position.
  我們公司的每個人都想相信我們在市場上仍居於首屈一指的地位。而事實上，我們與過去差得太遠了。

›› 還有這樣的表現方式

Everyone had expected that the new advertising strategy would have a positive response. **As a matter of fact**, it turned out to be as ineffective as the former one.

大家原本都期望新的廣告策略可以帶來正面的回應。而事實上，結果它跟之前的一樣無效。

除了 as a matter of fact，還可以用 in effect（事實上）/ actually（其實）。

XO Soft moved to the south to cut costs. Similarly, we need to do something to keep our costs low.

ＸＯ軟體為了減低成本搬去了南部。同樣的，我們也需要做點事來維持低成本。

這是使用比較語法 (comparing) 的句子，03 是將焦點放在 A 與 B 的差異，這裡則是將焦點放在 A 與 B 的相似點。

與其他事例做比較

- They decided to restructure their sales network to maintain their market share. Similarly, we have to do something to survive in the market.
  他們決定重整他們的銷售網絡以維持市占率。同樣的，我們也必須做點事好在市場上存活下來。

- See how they have recruited workers in the labor market. Now it is time for us to do similarly.
  看看他們如何在勞動市場上徵才。現在也是我們做同樣事的時候了。

除了 similarly 之外，也可以用 the same（同樣的事）或是 likewise（同樣地）。

›› 還有這樣的表現方式

The market has positively responded to their innovative design which is appealing to young people. **In the same way**, our design needs to be improved.
市場對他們吸引年輕人的創新設計有正面的回響。同樣地，我們的設計也需要改進。

Their aggressive advertising strategies have lead them to dominate the cosmetics market. **Likewise**, it is time for us to concentrate on advertising and P.R.
他們積極的廣告策略使得他們主導了化妝品的市場。同樣地，也是我們該聚焦在廣告和公關上的時候。

05 There are some things to consider in launching a fast food business, for example, the location of the shop.

在開展速食事業時有幾件事必須考慮，比方說店面的位置。

在陳述事實或主張時，如果能舉出具有實質意義的例子，就能更輕易的讓聽衆了解與接受。

舉例

- We need to talk about how to increase our market share, for example, low prices, policies, advertising strategies, and so on.
  我們需要談談如何增加市占率，比方說，低價、政策、廣告策略等等。

- Our applicants need motivation, for example, job security, promotion opportunities, better wages, and so on.
  我們的求職者需要動機，比方說，工作保障、晉升機會、更高的薪資等等。

for example 也可以換成具同義的 for instance。

》還有這樣的表現方式

Today, the Internet shopping market is dominated by companies **such as** Amazon, E-Bay, and Auction.

在今日，網路購物市場被亞馬遜、E-bay、Auction 等這些公司所支配。

06 The procedure is generally easy to follow.

這個流程一般來說很容易遵隨。

陳述主張時，將某種事實一般化的話，往往可以讓聽眾更容易產生同感並且接受。但是要記住，如果太頻繁的使用這種敘述方式，反而有可能造成反效果。

一般化

- So far, the response to our product has generally been rather poor.
  到目前為止，對於我們產品的反應一般來說都不是很好。
- Generally, we have done much better than our competitors expected.
  一般來說，我們的表現比我們競爭對手預期的要好得多。
- Generally, our new marketing strategies have had a positive affect on sales revenue.
  一般來說，我們新的行銷策略對銷售收入有正面的效果。

一般化的句子也可以用副詞 usually，或是副詞片語如 As a general rule / In general 來表現。

〉〉還有這樣的表現方式

On the whole, the introduction of TQM has helped to decrease defect rates.
整體來說，TQM（全面品質管理）的導入有助於降低產品的不良率。

隨堂測驗 A

請用提示的單字完成句子。

1 由於我們增加了廣告支出使得銷售量提升。
(thanks / our / are / sales / more / up / spending / to)

→ ______________________________ on advertising.

2 每個人都說那是不可能的，但是我們還是做到了。
(anyway / it / but / made / we)

→ Everybody said that it was impossible, ______________________________.

3 我們公司的每個人都想相信我們在市場上仍居於首屈一指的地位。而事實上，我們與過去差得太遠了。
(nowhere / are / fact / in / we / position / that / near)

→ Everybody in our company wants to believe that we are still number one in the market. ______________________________

4 看看他們如何在勞動市場上徵才。現在也是我們做同樣事的時候了。
(for / it / time / is / similarly / do / now / us / to)

→ See how they have recruited workers in the labor market.

____

5 在開展速食事業時有幾件事必須考慮，比方說店面的位置。
(the shop / for / of / example / the location)

→ There are some things to consider in launching a fast food business,

______________________________.

6 這個流程一般來說很容易遵隨。
(easy / generally / follow / to)

→ The procedure is ______________________________.

隨堂測驗 B

請參考中文提示完成簡報內容。

現在，我們需要的是**投資**管理階層的教育。

At this point, what we need is ①________ in the training of managers.

在 1997 年 IMF 所造成的困境**期間**，我們幾乎瀕臨破產邊緣，當時，除了我們的管理階層**誰**幫了我們？

②________ the tough times caused by the IMF Period in 1997, we were almost on the brink of bankruptcy. At that time, ③________ helped us out other than our managers?

*on the brink of: 瀕臨～

多虧有他們的犧牲與奉獻，我們公司才得以克服困境，並**成長**為一個現在市值一千萬美金的公司，2017 年的營業收入更預期會達到五百五十萬美金。

④________ ________ their dedication and sacrifice, our company overcame its difficulties and ⑤________ ________ to a $10 million company now with $5.5 million dollars in revenues forecast for 2017.

他們叫我們專注在中小規模、**一般來說常被忽略**的公司上。他們也堅信長期的顧客滿意度對我們的生存來說極為重要。

They asked us to focus on small to medium-sized companies, which have been ⑥________ ________. They also maintained that long-term customer satisfaction was critical to our survival.

我們遵循了他們的建議，結果就是，我們得以保有**事實上**是我們公司之基柱的忠實顧客。

We followed their advice, and as a result, we were able to retain our loyal customers who are, ⑦________ ________, the backbone of our company.

我相信**現在**是補償我們的管理階層的時候了。如何做呢？讓我們給他們一個使自己更進一步成長的機會。**舉例來說**，如果他們想的話就送他們出國進修。

I believe ⑧________ is the time to provide fair compensation to our managers. How? Let us give them a chance to develop themselves further. ⑨________ ________, let them go abroad to study if they want.

沒有人知道未來會發生什麼事。在我們有能力的時候要為最糟的狀況做好準備。當我們面對其他的困境時，**同樣的**，將會是我們的管理階層來拯救公司。

Nobody knows for sure what will happen in the future. We have to prepare for the worst while we can. When we face other difficulties, in ⑩________ ________ ________, it will be our managers who will save our company.

我想說的就是，我們的人力就是我們的資產之一。

My point is that one of our assets is our manpower.

Bonus

使用視覺資料時要注意的事

1. 不要太頻繁的使用視覺資料。
2. 不要照著視覺資料念，要抓住簡報時需要的部分來說明。
3. 不要在視覺資料裡放入太多資訊。
4. 要適當的使用色彩，但是注意不要太過頭。
5. 一定要帶上雷射筆。
6. 要確認聽眾是否真的理解視覺資料。
7. 要用視覺資料來支持或概括簡報者的主張。
8. 能用話來說明的情報就避免用視覺資料。
9. 要考慮怎樣的視覺資料（graph / table / chart / picture 等）最適合簡報者。
10. 不要一直將視線放在視覺資料上，要盡可能地面對聽眾。
11. 簡報者必須小心不要遮到聽眾觀看視覺資料的視線。

隨堂測驗 A

1 Sales are up thanks to our spending more 2 but we made it anyway
3 In fact, we are nowhere near that position. 4 Now it is time for us to do similarly.
5 for example, the location of the shop 6 generally easy to follow

隨堂測驗 B

① investment ② During ③ who ④ Thanks to ⑤ has grown
⑥ generally ignored ⑦ in fact ⑧ now ⑨ For example[instance] ⑩ the same way

Week 2 複習時間

A. 使用下面的單字完成句子。

exceeds	illustrate	from	fact	slight
as	and	somewhere	demand	

1 Let me ________ this point with some statistical data.
讓我用幾個數據資料來說明這一點。

2 ________ you can see ________ this pie chart, our profit margin takes up a very small portion.
各位可以從這個圓餅圖看出，我們的利潤只占了非常小的一部分。

3 There has been a ________ gain in our market share.
我們的市占率有微幅的成長。

4 Our total costs for this month are expected to be ________ between 50,000 ________ 60,000 dollars.
我們這個月的總成本預計大約會在五到六萬美金之間。

5 In ________, there is still a chance for us.
事實上，我們還是有機會的。

6 The ________ for organic foods ________ the supply.
有機食品的需求超過供給。

B. 使用提示句完成下列句子。

1 請各位注意這個格子裡的數字。

Hint concentrate on

→ ______________________________

2 看這個圖，我們就可以了解產品是怎樣送到顧客那裡的。

Hint look at / we see how ~

→ ______________________________

3 我們的利潤在夏天有了成長。

Hint go up / have p.p.

→ ______________________________

4 上個月的通貨膨脹率觸底。

Hint bottomed out

→ ______________________________

5 這項投資使得我們公司資金短缺。

Hint leave + 受詞 + short of

→ ______________________________

6 同樣的，我們的設計也需要改進。

Hint similarly

→ ______________________________

C. 根據提示完成下面簡報的空格。 MP3 18

1

Now, why don't we ________ ________ this graph? It ________ the consumption of milk over the past five years. On ________ ________ ________, you see milk consumption measured in tons, while ________ ________ ________ measures years.

現在，我們何不看看這個圖表。它顯示了過去五年牛奶的消費量。垂直軸以「噸」來計算牛奶的消費量，水平軸則為年度消費量。

2

I'd like to draw ________ ________ ________ the two lines here.
The solid line ________ our turnover, while the ________ ________ represents our profits. As you can see from this graph, our turnover has ________ ________ over the last five years. However, our profits have steadily ________ over the same period.
How can this be explained? ________ the reason for this, we will soon be in the red unless we do something immediately.

我想請各位注意這兩條線。實線代表我們的總營業額，虛線則是我們的利潤。各位可以從這個圖表看出，過去五年來我們的總營業額有穩定地成長，但是，同一時期我們的利潤則持續地減少。
這該如何解釋？不管原因為何，除非我們立刻改進，要不然很快就會出現赤字。

3

________ at the graph, we see that our productivity reached ________ ________ last year. Accordingly, there has been a dramatic ________ in our profitability during the same period. Profits stood at a staggering 20 million dollars, which is ________ ________ our expectations.

看這個表，我們可以了解我們的產量在去年達到最高點。因此，同一時期我們的利潤也有相當的增加，當時的利潤數字達到令人驚訝的兩千萬美金，遠遠超過了我們的預期。

Answers

A 1 illustrate 2 As / from 3 slight 4 somewhere / and 5 fact 6 demand / exceeds

B 1 I'd like us to concentrate on the figure in this box.
2 Looking at this diagram, we see how the product is delivered to our customers.
3 Our profits have gone up during the summer.
4 Inflation rates bottomed out last month.
5 This investment has left our company short of money.
6 Similarly, our design needs to be improved.

C 1 look at / shows / the vertical axis / the horizontal axis
2 your attention to / represents / dotted line / steadily increased / decreased / Whatever
3 Looking / its peak / gain[growth / increase] / well over

Week 3

進行篇②

星期六第一堂課 有效果的簡報表現方式 (1)

星期六第二堂課 有效果的簡報表現方式 (2)

星期日第一堂課 強調 (1)

星期日第二堂課 強調 (2)

複習時間

Week

3 有效果的簡報表現方式 (1)

It seems we will have to delay the delivery.

| 星期六第一堂課 |

〉〉跟著崔副理一起看看如何用有效果的表現方式來進行簡報的主體 (body)。

有效果的簡報方式

附加

此外，我們有技術的優勢。

Plus, we have the advantage of technology.

提出證據

根據廣泛的研究調查，我認為我們應該～

Based on extensive research, I think we should ~.

說明出處

按照企業計畫，毛利率將會增加～

According to the business plan, gross margin will increase ~.

Kate 老師的重點提示

□ **按照～，依據～ according to** 用來「說明出處」或「引用」，to 後面接人或是報章雜誌等「出處」。

□ **此外 moreover** 用於在前面敘述過的事情上附加說明，與 what's more / in addition 同義。

□ **多樣化 diversify** 一般常用來形容「分散」事業投資對象跟事業的「多樣化」。

□ **獲益 benefit** 後面用 from 或是 by，說明獲益的來源。

□ **妥協，折衷 compromise** come to a compromise 就是「達成妥協」的意思，「在 B 這件事上與 A 達成妥協」可說成 compromise with A over B。

□ **執行 execute** 意為「執行」某項職務或命令，與 carry out 同義。

□ **划算 pay** 雖然這個字基本上是「付出報酬」的意思，但也可以用來形容某種行動或物品「帶來效益」。

□ **基於，根據～ be based on**

委婉的主張

看來我們得延遲出貨。

It seems we'll have to delay the delivery.

提出問題

現在的問題是「要如何～」。

The issue here is how to ~.

和緩內容

我們在市場上的聲譽並不是那麼令人鼓舞。

Our reputation in the market is *not* very *encouraging*.

Key Expressions 6

簡報的目的之一是要堅持主張，所以必須掌握「如何提出證據出處」、「如何和緩內容」，以及「如何附加說明」的表達方式。

MP3 19

01 Based on extensive research, I think we should diversify our products.

根據廣泛的研究調查，我認為我們應該讓產品更多樣化。

替自己的主張提出證據或是實質的根據，會讓簡報內容更值得信賴，以下是相關的表現方式。

提出證據

- Based on recent statistics, we can predict that sales of organic foods will grow.
  根據最近的統計資料，我們可以預期有機食品的銷量將會增加。
- Based on the recent reposts by the media, we think that the brand will eventually lose its power in our industry.
  根據最近的媒體報導，我們認為該品牌最終會在我們的產業失去影響力。

›› 還有這樣的表現方式

This plan has been created **on the basis of** five years of market research.
這個計畫是根據五年的市場調查所訂出來的。

Our projected sales figures for next year have been decided **on the basis of** sales revenues for the last five years.
我們明年度的預計銷售數字是根據過去五年的銷售收入所訂出來的。

02 According to the directions on the label, you should avoid breathing the spray mist.

按照標籤上的指示，你應該避免吸入噴霧。

當要引用他人或是媒體的情報和想法時，一定要確實地說明出處。

說明資訊的出處

- According to Schultz's theory, individuals join groups in part to satisfy three needs: inclusion, control, and affection.
  按照舒茲的理論，個人會加入團體在某種程度上是為了滿足三個需求：歸屬感、控制慾，以及情感。

- According to the article which appeared in the September 8, 2002, issue of *The Economist*, companies are switching from producing products to marketing images.
  依據 2002 年九月八日《經濟學人》雜誌上的一篇文章，很多公司正在由製造產品轉移到行銷形象上。

- According to the business plan, the gross margin will increase to 80% by the third year of operations.
  依據該企業計畫，我們的毛利率在營運的第三年將會增加到 80%。

›› 還有這樣的表現方式

I **quote** our CEO **as saying that** we will increase the promotion budget by 20%.
讓我重複執行長說過的，我們將會增加 20% 的促銷預算。

03 Plus, we have the advantage of technology.

此外，我們有技術的優勢。

Plus 這個副詞是用於附加情報至前面說過的內容，也是一種強調語法，強調在 plus 後面出現的內容。下面是另外幾個可以用來附加情報的表達方式。

附加說明

- Above all, we need renovations.
  最重要的是，我們需要革新。
- What's more, the economic situation in Japan is gradually recovering.
  更重要的是，日本的經濟狀況正逐漸改善中。
- In addition, we don't have any funds available.
  此外，我們沒有任何可以使用的資金。
- In particular, we need to invest in our employees.
  尤其是，我們需要投資在員工身上。
- On top of that, the birth rate of our country has been gradually decreasing.
  最重要的是，我國的生育率正逐漸下降中。
- Moreover, M&As in the banking industry have been continuing.
  此外，銀行業的併購一直在持續中。

04 It seems we will have to delay the delivery.

看來我們得延遲出貨。

雖然有時針對某事直接下斷言會很有效果，但是有些時候，若將確信的程度減低，以較委婉的方式來表達會更具說服力。用到動詞 seem 的語句帶有保留其他可能性的語氣，可以說是一種安全裝置，也是顯示說話者謙遜的一種表達方式。

委婉的說明事實與主張

- Our competitor seems to dominate the market.
  看來是我們的競爭者在主導市場。
- It seems that we need to look for ways to compromise.
  看來我們需要想辦法妥協。
- Linda seems to have many ideas about investing our money.
  琳達似乎有很多關於如何投資我們資金的想法。

›› 還有這樣的表現方式

There appears to be increasing support for the new project.
新計畫似乎得到愈來愈多的支持。

I tend to think we should stop investing now.
我傾向認為現在我們應該停止投資。

Some other possibilities **might** be worth considering.
其他的可能性似乎也值得考慮。

助動詞 might 的語感比強烈勸告的 must / should 來的委婉。

05 Our reputation in the market is not very encouraging.

我們在市場上的聲譽並不是那麼令人鼓舞。

因考慮到聽者的心情而想要採取較為間接和緩的表現方式時，可以選擇使用否定詞 not 的說法。上面這個句子就是用 not very encouraging 取代直接的 disappointing，讓語氣變得較為和緩。

和緩語氣

- The CEO is going to be furious.
  執行長會很生氣。

  → The CEO isn't going to be very happy.
  執行長可能會不太高興。

- Your offer is much too expensive.
  你的報價太高了。

  → Your offer is not as low as we had expected.
  你的報價沒有我們預期的低。

也可以用副詞來緩和語氣。比方說 sometimes（有時候）／ a little（稍微）／ probably（可能）／ rather（多少）／ all in all（總之）／ just about（大約）／ to some extent（某種程度上）等等。

›› 還有這樣的表現方式

We're going to reduce our workforce **a bit**.
我們要稍微減少一些人力。

To some extent, it is true.
某種程度上來說，那是真的。

Perhaps you should consider resigning.
或許你該考慮辭職。

06 The issue here is how to encourage members to make a greater effort.

現在的問題是要如何鼓勵同仁更加努力。

「提出問題」也是在簡報時可以聚焦的一種策略，主詞的位置除了 The issue 之外，也可以用 The question、The problem 或是 The thing。

提出問題

- The issue here is that the prices for crucial raw materials keep soaring.
  現在的問題是至關重要的原物料價格不斷地上漲。
- The issue here is that our security system has been hacked.
  現在的問題是我們的保全系統已經被駭了。

›› 還有這樣的表現方式

The question we are facing is whether or not we need new leadership for our company.
現在我們所面臨的問題是公司需不需要新的領導階層。

The problem at hand is that our employees are resisting changes.
現在的問題是我們的員工在抗拒改變。

The thing is that we are not a market leader.
問題是我們並非市場領導者。

這邊的 the thing 意味著 the important fact[idea]。

隨堂測驗 A

請用提示的單字完成句子。

1 根據最近的統計資料，我們可以預期有機食品的銷量將會增加。
(statistics / on / based / recent)

→ ________________, we can predict that sales of organic foods will grow.

2 按照該企業計畫，我們的毛利率在營運的第三年將會增加到 80%。
(plan / according / the / to / business)

→ ________________, the gross margin will increase to 80% by the third year of operations.

3 此外，我們有技術的優勢。
(have / technology / we / plus / of / the / advantage)

→ ________________

4 看來我們需要想辦法妥協。
(that / seems / to / it / we / need)

→ ________________ look for ways to compromise.

5 我們在市場上的聲譽並不是那麼令人鼓舞。
(very / not / is / encouraging)

→ Our reputation in the market ________________.

6 現在的問題是我們的員工在抗拒改變。
(problem / hand / is / at / that / the)

→ ________________ our employees are resisting changes.

B 請參考中文提示完成簡報內容。

按照神奇行銷顧問公司所做的市調，近年來對統計資料的需求有顯著的增加。

① ________ ________ the market research done by Magic Marketing Consultants, there has been a significant increase in the demand for statistical data in recent years.

這意味著許多公司是**根據**他們蒐集到的數據在計畫與進行事業活動。

This means that many companies plan and execute their business ② ________ ________ the numbers they have gathered.

他們想知道他們有興趣投資之地區的人口統計資訊。他們想知道**有多少**人住在該區域，這些數據是如何地隨時間改變等等。

They want to know the demographic statistics in an area they want to invest. They want to know ③ ________ ________ people live there, how these figures vary over time and so on.

*demographic：人口（統計）學

這些資料能協助企業計畫者們**決定**市場的大小、成長以及顧客需求，甚至是購買的行為模式。

The data help the business planners ④ ________ ________ the size and growth of the market and customer needs, and even buying behavior trends.

看來資料分析最終是值得的。按照神奇行銷的調查，八成的公司表示他們在開始新事業時的確有從分析上獲益。

⑤________ ________ that data analysis ultimately pays off. According to the Magic Marketing research, eight out of ten companies responded that they had benefited from ⑥________ ________ when they started a new business.

*pay off：得到效益；付全額

現在的問題是資料就是金錢，所以，我們或許可以考慮將販售資料當作下一個事業項目。

⑦________ ________ ________ is that data is money. So, selling data might be worth considering as our next business item.

如果這樣的話，我們要販售怎樣的資料？此外，我們要如何知道怎樣的公司需要怎樣的統計資料？

If so, what kind of data do we have to sell? ⑧________ ________, how do we know which companies need which statistics?

Answers

隨堂測驗 A

1 Based on recent statistics 2 According to the business plan
3 Plus, we have the advantage of technology. 4 It seems that we need to
5 is not very encouraging 6 The problem at hand is that

隨堂測驗 B

① According to ② based on ③ how many ④ to decide ⑤ It seems ⑥ data analysis
⑦ The issue here ⑧ In addition

Bonus

簡報時可以利用的表現方法

1. **As things stand**, we can't pay off all of our bank loans.
在這樣的狀況下，我們沒有辦法付清所有的銀行貸款。

2. **At the most**, we can make barely enough money to buy raw materials from overseas markets.
最多，我們也只能勉強賺到從海外市場購買原物料的錢。

3. **At least**, we did not lose our money although we did not make a profit.
至少，我們沒有賠錢，雖然沒有賺到錢。

4. **In other words**, the company has the best customer service network in the industry.
換句話說，該公司有業界最好的客服網。

5. **At any rate**, our sales are holding steady in spite of the fact that we are new to the market.
不論如何，縱使我們才剛進入市場，我們的銷售卻很穩定。

6. You don't have to worry about slow sales in overseas markets. **As a last resort**, we can rely on the domestic market where we still enjoy strong sales.
你不需要擔心海外市場的銷售力道不足。**在萬不得已的時候**，我們至少可以依賴我們在國內市場上依舊強勁的銷售量。

7. Last year, our workforce was cut in half thanks to a restructuring plan. **As a direct result**, working hours have been prolonged and job performance is disappointing.
去年，我們的人力因為重整計畫而減半。**導致的結果就是**，工時變長而且工作成果令人失望。

8. **Under the right conditions**, we can make profits in the Japanese market.
狀況好的話，我們在日本市場上可以獲利。

Week

3

有效果的簡報表現方式 (2)

What differentiates this product from others is its durability.

| 星期六第二堂課 |

〉〉跟著崔副理一起看看可以增進理解並且說服聽衆的表現方法。

有效果的簡報方式

提出關聯性

產量的增加與～有密切的關係。

Increased production is closely related to ~.

講出目標達成方案

如果～，我們就可以達成目標。

We can reach our goal if ~.

具體說明

我們將會提高預算，更明確地說，就是～的錢。

We will increase our budget, to be more specific, the money for ~.

Kate 老師的重點提示

- □ **詳細地、具體地 specifically** 也可以用 to be more specific 來表達。
- □ **與～有差別 differentiate from** 將要比較的對象放在 from 的後面，distinguish from 也是同樣的意思。
- □ **與～有關 be related to** 若要說明「與～有密切的關係」，則加副詞 closely，即 be closely related to。
- □ **達成目標 reach one's goal** 動詞也可以用 achieve / attain。
- □ **獎勵、刺激、動機 incentive** 一般公司所謂的獎勵薪資制度 (incentive wage system) 是指達到一定成果就給付紅利的一種「誘發動機」制度。
- □ **考慮全局後 all things considered** consider 是「考慮、考量」的意思，這個結構常被用來形容綜合考量各種要素後得到結論的狀況。
- □ **力促～去努力 urge** urge A to do something 就是「強烈鼓勵 A 去～」的意思。

講出優缺點

我們產品的優點是～；缺點是～。

The strength of our product is ~; the weakness is ~.

強烈的陳述意見

我相信我們必須～。

I believe that we have to ~.

提出差別

A 與 B 的差別在於～。

What differentiate A from B is ~.

Key Expressions 6

在簡報當中欲提出想法或是傳遞情報時，列出優缺點、差別點、關聯性，或是舉出具體事例來說明等等，都是可以增進理解、說服聽眾的有效方法。

01 The strength of our product includes its cheap price; the only weakness is its design.

我們產品的優點包括了價格便宜；唯一的缺點就是設計。

講到簡報主題、想法或是某樣產品時，如果能均衡地介紹出優缺點，會讓簡報者更讓人信賴。以下是幾種介紹優缺點的方法。

點出優缺點

- The strength of building a factory in China is that we can expect cost cuts in many areas; the weakness is that we may have difficulties in managing workers because of communication and culture barriers.
  在中國開工廠的優點是很多方面都能降低成本；缺點則是可能會因為溝通與文化上的隔閡而在管理員工時遇到困難。

›› 還有這樣的表現方式

We will discuss **the advantages and disadvantages** of setting up a new company.
我們將討論開設新公司的好處和壞處。

We can debate **the merits and demerits** of the business plan.
我們可以討論這個企業計畫的優缺點。

The pros and cons of this project will be debated at a meeting.
這個計畫的利與弊將會在會議中討論。

除了這些之外，也可以用 the pluses and minuses（得失）來表示優缺點或優劣勢。

02

We need to concentrate on the South, to be more specific, Tainan, Kaohsiung, and Pingtung.

我們必須著力在南部，明確來說，就是台南、高雄及屏東。

在進行具體且詳細的說明時，可以用 for example, for instance 或是 specifically, particularly 這些詞語來表現。

具體詳細的說明

- We will increase our budget, to be more specific, the money for the welfare of our employees.
  我們會增加預算，更明確地說，就是員工福利的錢。
- We will meet to discuss these issues, to be more specific, the goal of the team and the needs of individuals.
  我們會開會來討論這些問題，更明確地說，就是團隊目標與個人的需求。

›› 還有這樣的表現方式

We need to **specifically** target female consumers.
我們需要特別針對女性消費者。

When we select a new server management company, we **particularly** consider experience in the industry and price.
我們在選擇新的伺服器管理公司時，會特別考慮業界的經驗跟價格。

03 What differentiates this product from others is its durability.

這個產品與其他產品的差別就在耐用性上。

在說明自家產品或是服務的特點時，一定要跟其他同類的產品或服務做比較，以凸顯自家產品更優異的地方。這時可以用 What differentiates A form B is ~（A與B的差別就在於～）。

提出差別

- What differentiates our TV advertising from other is that Claymation has been used for the first time in this industry.
  我們的電視廣告跟其他廣告的差別在於，黏塑動畫在這個業界是首次被使用。
- What sets this digital camera apart from other similar products is that it is waterproof.
  這個數位相機跟其他類似產品的差別就在於它防水。
- What makes our product distinguishable from others is its user-friendly design concept.
  我們產品跟其他產品的不同就在於它易於使用的設計概念。

也可以用動詞來表達：
make A distinguish from B。

›› 還有這樣的表現方式

Let me explain the new features that **differentiate** them **from** the old ones.
讓我說明一下這些與既有產品不同的新特性。

Cyberspace makes it difficult to **differentiate between** the imaginative world **and** the real world.
網路空間讓人難以區分想像世界與真實世界。

Increased production is closely related to incentives such as promotion and bonuses.

產量的增加與升遷及紅利這些獎勵措施有密切的關係。

說明 A 與 B 的關聯性時，可以用 A is related to B，或是 There is a connection between A and B 來表示。

點出關聯性

- A country's political situation is closely related to its economic situation.
  一個國家的政治狀況與它的經濟狀況有密切的關係。

- The increase in our sales revenue is closely related to the increased advertising budget.
  我們銷售收益的增長與廣告預算的增加有密切的關係。

- The increase in our annual revenue is closely related to the expansion of our overseas subsidiaries.
  我們年度收益的增加與海外分公司的擴張有密切的關係。

〉〉還有這樣的表現方式

Our success **has to do with** our R&D budget, which has increased every year.
我們的成功與每年增加的研發預算有關。

The adoption of a new system **has to do with** reducing surplus stocks and storage costs.
改用新系統與減少多餘庫存及倉儲成本有關。

05 I believe that we should urge our group to beat its previous record.

我認為我們應該力促我們的團隊打破先前的紀錄。

要強力表明自己的意見時，可以用 I believe that ~（我認為~）來強調，但要以合理的根據為基礎，有邏輯地來陳述。

強調主張

- I believe that we could act without consulting marketing agencies.
  我認為我們不需要行銷企劃公司的幫助就可以行動。
- I believe that we have to take action right away.
  我認為我們必須立刻採取行動。
- I believe that we have to reorganize our database immediately.
  我認為我們必須立即重整資料庫。

›› 還有這樣的表現方式

I feel that this new product will give us a chance to be a market leader.
我覺得這個新產品將讓我們有機會成為市場領導者。

I think that we need to secure the funds right away.
我認為我們需要立刻獲得資金。

06 We can reach our goal if we work very hard for it.

如果我們非常努力就可以達成目標。

表達「如果我們～就可以達成目標」的 We can reach our goal if we ~ 是簡報做結論時很好用的句子。也可以用 achieve / attain 來取代 reach。

做結論

- We can reach our goal if we eliminate defects from the production.
  如果我們排除生產上的缺陷就可以達成目標。
- We can reach our goal if we involve experienced staff members in this project.
  如果我們讓有經驗的員工參與這個計畫，我們就可以達成目標。
- We can reach our goal if we focus on a niche market with high-priced products.
  如果我們用高價產品聚焦在利基市場上，我們就可以達成目標。

›› 還有這樣的表現方式

Our recommendation is that we turn to niche marketing.
我們的建議是轉向利基市場行銷。

My suggestion is that we test the market before launching our product.
我的建議是我們在推出新產品之前先測試市場。

也可以用 Our recommendation is ~ 或是 My suggestion is ~ 來闡明自己的主張。

隨堂測驗 A

請用提示的單字完成句子。

1 我們產品的優點包括了價格便宜；唯一的缺點就是設計。
(its / the / weakness / only / is / design)
→ The strength of our product includes its cheap price;
____________________________________.

2 我們需要著力在南部，更明確地說，就是台南、高雄及屏東。
(be / specific / more / to)
→ We need to concentrate on the South, __________________________ Tainan, Kaohsiung, and Pingtung.

3 這個產品與其他產品的差別就在耐用性上。
(this / from / differentiates / what / others / product)
→ ____ is its durability.

4 一個國家的政治狀況與它的經濟狀況有密切的關係。
(economic / its / related / closely / to / situation)
→ A country's political situation is __________________________________.

5 我認為我們必須立刻採取行動。
(believe / action / I / we / take / that / to / have)
→ ____ right away.

6 如果我們排除生產上的缺陷就可以達成目標。
(goal / can / if / reach / we / our)
→ _____________________________ we eliminate defects from the production.

隨堂測驗 B

請參考中文提示完成簡報內容。

我們將會開發一個線上遊戲來吸引目標客群，**更明確地說**，就是八到十二歲的兒童。

We will make an online game that appeals to the target market, to ①________ ________ ________, children aged 8-12.

這個網路遊戲**與**其他線上遊戲**的差別**就在教育價值，這點明確地能夠吸引目標客層的父母與教育人士。

②________ ________ this web-based game ③________ other online games are its educational value, which will appeal specifically to the parents and educators of the target market.

它的教育價值，簡單來說，與發展年幼孩童的創意心智**有密切的關係**。

Its educational values, briefly put, are ④________ ________ ________ developing the creative minds of young children.

這個線上遊戲的**優點**是具競爭力的價格、教育娛樂性，以及不會讓新手卻步的遊戲環境；不過**缺點**就是目標市場太小，畢竟我們只以年輕孩童為目標。

⑤________ ________ of this online game are its competitive price, its edutainment values, and a game environment that won't intimidate novice users; ⑥________ ________ , however, is the limited target market, because we are targeting only young children.

考慮全局之後，這是一個值得考慮的計畫。

All things considered, this is a project worth considering.

我相信我們未來的顧客會花錢在孩子身上，**因為**他們會欣賞我們將要開發的線上遊戲。

I believe our future clients will spend money on their children ⑦________ they will appreciate the online game that we will create.

我相信我們能**達到**主導網路遊戲產業的**目標**，如果能讓我們開始這個計畫的話。

I am sure we can ⑧________ ________ ________ – to dominate the Internet game industry – if we are allowed to start this project.

隨堂測驗 A

1 the only weakness is its design 2 to be more specific,
3 What differentiates this product from others 4 closely related to its economic situation
5 I believe that we have to take action 6 We can reach our goal if

隨堂測驗 B

① be more specific ② What differentiates ③ from ④ closely related to ⑤ The strengths
⑥ the weakness ⑦ because ⑧ reach our goal

Bonus

委婉的商業用語

在簡報時，最好可以考慮聽者的感覺，多用美化過的字詞委婉地傳達想法，比方說用「環境美化人員」代替「清潔工」，用「去洗個手」代替「去上廁所」。下面是幾個跟商業活動有關的委婉用語。

實際的意思	委婉的說法
industrial espionage 商業間諜	competitor analysis 競爭者分析
tax evasion 避稅	income protection 收益保障
secretary 祕書	personal assistant 個人助理 administrative assistant 行政助理
presenting oneself or one's product in the best possible light 呈現個人或是產品最好的一面	public relations 公關宣傳
money lending 借錢	financial services 金融服務
a part of the economy consisting of money that has been earned but on which, illegally, no tax has been paid 賺錢不繳稅的非法經濟活動	black economy 地下經濟
money 錢	resources / funds / finances 資源／基金／財務金融
unemployed 失業	between jobs 轉職中
relieve someone of their duties / someone's services are no longer required 解僱／工作上不再需要某人	early retirement 提前退休
losing money 賠錢	a temporary cash-flow problem 暫時的現金周轉問題
bankrupt 破產	fold / go under / close its door 停業，關門
economic contraction may not seem so serious 經濟萎縮也許不是那麼嚴重	negative growth 負成長

Week

3

| 星期日第一堂課 |

強調 (1)

Obviously, we lost an opportunity.

〉〉跟著崔副理一起看看在做簡報時該如何強調意見或主張。

強調的表現方式

使用片語 not ~ until ...

我直到今天才了解這有多麼重要。

I didn't realize this was so important until today.

用副詞強調整個句子

很清楚地，這對我們來說是個好兆頭。

Clearly, this is a good sign for us.

用講反話的方式來強調

我們怎樣強調～的重要也不為過。

We can't emphasize the importance of ~ too much.

Kate 老師的重點提示

- □ **重要的** **important** 表達同樣意思的形容詞還有 significant / crucial 等，例如在說明重點時可以用 What is important is ~（重要的是）作為一個句子的開頭。
- □ **使變長，延長** **prolong** 是「加長、延長」長度或時間的意思，與 extend 同義，比方說 prolong one's stay abroad（延長海外居留時間）。
- □ **關鍵性的，重大的** **critical** a critical situation 就是會給日後帶來影響的「重大狀況」，critical 也有「危機的、危急的」意思。
- □ **斷然地，直截了當地** **categorically** 形容詞 categorical 是「無條件、絕對」的意思，例如 categorically refuse 是「斷然地拒絕」，更確實地強調拒絕的心意。
- □ **承認** **admit** 特別帶有承認不好的事情的語感。
- □ **總收入，所得總額** **revenues** revenue 用來指稅收或是一般收入，只有複數型 revenues 是「總收入、所得總額」的意思。
- □ **有成本效益的** **cost-effective** 也可以說 cost-efficient，就是生產效益比投資費用高的意思。

用副詞來強調動詞

我們強烈的建議～

We strongly recommend that ~.

關係代名詞 what

尤其重要的是～。

What is especially important is ~.

強調最重要的點

或許最重要的是～。

Probably most important of all is/are ~.

Key Expressions 6

「強調」也是簡報時最常用來確實表明自己主張或想法的方法，接著就來看看各種強調的說法。

MP3 23

01 I didn't realize this was so important until today.

我直到今天才了解這有多麼重要。

「否定句」可以用來強調某種事實或主張。not ~ unitl ... 直譯為「不～直到～」，也就是「直到～才～」的意思，間接地表示終於體悟了某種過去不知道的重要事情。

體悟重要事情

- I didn't realize this was so important until I got complaints from our customers.
  我直到接到客戶的抱怨才了解這有多麼重要。
- I didn't realize this was so important until the media reported on it.
  我直到媒體報導才了解這有多麼重要。
- I didn't realize this was so important until our share of the market started dwindling.
  我直到我們的市占率開始下降了才了解這有多麼重要。

dwindle 和 decrease / diminish / lesson / fall 一樣，都有「減少、衰退」的意思。

›› 還有這樣的表現方式

I clearly **understand** the importance of managing employees **after** having failed in my venture business.
我是直到創業失敗才清楚地了解員工管理的重要。

02 What is especially important is our patience.

尤其重要的是我們的耐心。

強調重要事實或主張時，可以用 what 當主詞，先抓住聽眾的注意力，然後再強調後面的內容。

用 what 來強調

- What is especially important is that we have to secure the land.
  尤其重要的是我們必須取得土地。
- What is especially important is prolonging the period of the project.
  尤其重要的是要延長專案的時間。
- What is especially important is understanding the culture of the immigrant workers.
  尤其重要的是要了解外籍移工的文化。

›› 還有這樣的表現方式

What I'd like to do is (to) look at this problem from a different perspective.
我想做的是從另一個角度看這個問題。

What we want to do is (to) build a new factory.
我們要做的是開設新的工廠。

What we can't afford to do is (to) spend too much on advertising.
我們沒有辦法負擔的是花太多錢在廣告上。

上面這個句子就是使用 what 來 強調 We can't afford to spend too much on advertising（我們付不起太多廣告費）。在這種 What + 主詞 + do is ~ 或是 All + 主詞 + do is 的句子裡，主詞後面的動詞用原型或是「不定詞 to + 原型」都可以。

03 We strongly believe that this method is cost-effective.

我們強烈認為這個方法是有成本效益的。

句子的核心在動詞，所以如果在動詞前面加上有強調意味的副詞，就可以更強烈地傳達句子的信息。

用副詞來強調 ①

- We deeply regret that we did not meet the deadline.
  我們對於沒有趕上期限深感遺憾。
- We totally reject your final offer.
  我們完全拒絕你的最終報價。
- We fully admit that our service is not to your satisfaction.
  我們完全承認我們的服務不是令您滿意的。
- We sincerely hope that you have enjoyed our services.
  我們真誠地希望您喜歡我們的服務。
- We categorically deny your accusations.
  我們絕對地否認你的指控。

04 Obviously, we lost an opportunity.

很明顯地，我們錯過了一次機會。

將副詞放在句子開頭的話，這個副詞可以修飾整個句子。如果用否定的副詞，整個句子就會是否定的；如果用帶有強調意味的副詞，就可以強調整個句子要傳遞的信息。

用副詞來強調 ②

- Evidently, we are losing money this year.
  很明顯地，我們今年在賠錢。

- Clearly, this is a good sign for us.
  很清楚地，這對我們來說是好的兆頭。

›› 還有這樣的表現方式

＊ 將強調副詞放在形容詞前就可以強調那個形容詞。

We've had an **extremely** good year.
我們有了非常好的一年。

That is a **positively** encouraging sign.
那是一個絕對令人鼓舞的徵兆。

That is an **absolutely** fantastic offer.
那是一個極佳的提議。

Yours is an **entirely** wrong set of figures.
你的那組數字是完全錯誤的。

05 We can't emphasize the importance of the workforce too much.

我們怎樣強調人力的重要也不為過。

can't emphasize ~ too much 直譯是「不能強調～更多」，意即再怎麼強調也不會過頭，是美式的強調語法。

用講反話的方式來強調

- I can't emphasize enough just how critical this is.
  我怎樣強調這點多麼關鍵都不為過。
- I can't stress this enough.
  我怎樣強調這點都不為過。
- I can't emphasize the importance of honesty too much.
  我怎樣強調誠實的重要性都不為過。

>> 還有這樣的表現方式

The importance of a logo **can't be emphasized enough**.
商標的重要性怎樣強調都不為過。

06 Probably most important of all are customer relationships.

或許最重要的是客戶關係。

most important of all is / are ~ 是在列舉幾個主要事項之後，用來強調其中最重要部分的表達方式。在這句中加上帶有謙虛語感的 probably，可以讓強調的語氣更有效果。

強調最重要的點

- Probably most important of all are **our working conditions.**
  或許最重要的是我們的工作情況。
- Probably most important of all are **our marketing strategies.**
  或許最重要的是我們的行銷策略。
- Probably most important of all is **our determination to make it.**
  或許最重要的是我們想做到的決心。

›› 還有這樣的表現方式

Speeding up the development of a new product is **of paramount importance**.
加快新產品開發是極為重要的。

Increasing production is **of paramount importance**.
增加產能是極為重要的。

of paramount importance 意同於 extremely important，這裡的 paramount 即「最高、最重要」之意。

隨堂測驗 A

請用提示的單字完成句子。

1 我直到今天才了解這有多麼重要。
(important / this / so / didn't / realize / until / was)

→ I ______________________________ today.

2 尤其重要的是我們必須取得土地。
(especially / is / what / important / is)

→ ______________________________ that we have to secure the land.

3 我們強烈認為這個方法是有成本效益的。
(that / we / believe / strongly)

→ ______________________________ this method is cost-effective.

4 很明顯地，我們今年在賠錢。
(are / money / evidently / losing / we)

→ ______________________________ this year.

5 我們怎樣強調人力的重要也不為過。
(importance / we / can't / emphasize / the)

→ ______________________________ of the workforce too much.

6 或許最重要的是客戶關係。
(most / all / probably / important / of)

→ ______________________________ are customer relationships.

隨堂測驗 B

請參考中文提示完成簡報內容。

我們**強烈**推薦您選擇新竹作為您的廠址。讓我跟您說明為什麼您應該選擇台灣的這個地區。

We ①________ recommend Hsinchu as the location of your facility. Let me tell you why you should choose this part of Taiwan.

首先讓我們談談地理上的要素。新竹離國道一號很近，坐車**一個小時之內**就可以到台北，開車到台灣的門戶桃園機場也只要 45 分鐘。

Let's first talk about the geographical factor. Hsinchu is located near the National Highway No. 1, which will take you to Taipei ②________ ________ ________ by car, and only a 45-minute drive from Taoyuan Airport, a gateway of Taiwan.

我**怎樣強調**這對設立新工廠來說有多重要**都不為過**。

I ③________ ________ ________ just how important this is in selecting a site for your factory.

其次是基礎建設。這個城市的通信與交通建設都非常完備。(……)

Second, infrastructure. The city is well-equipped with a communication and transportation infrastructure. (...)

第三就是人。**很明顯地**，沒有人力是沒有辦法做生意的。我們這邊有許多有經驗又受過良好教育而且完全符合資格的人員。(……)

Third, people. ④________, you can't do business without a workforce. Here, we have lots of experienced, well-educated, and well-qualified workers. (...)

最後，是地方政府的稅務政策。**或許最重要的**就是您在這邊開展事業的話能省下多少稅。

Lastly, the local government's tax policies. ⑤________ ________ ________ of all is how much you can save in taxes if you start your business here in Hsinchu.

新竹市議會已經通過了幾項專門為協助外國投資人的新法令。其中**最重要的改變**是減免外國創投的房地產稅。

The Hsinchu City Council has already passed several laws that have been designed to help foreign investors. One of the ⑥________ ________ ________ is property-tax exemptions for foreign venture capital.

Answers

隨堂測驗 A

1 didn't realize this was so important until 2 What is especially important is
3 We strongly believe that 4 Evidently, we are losing money
5 We can't emphasize the importance 6 Probably most important of all

隨堂測驗 B

① strongly ② within one hour ③ can't emphasize enough ④ Obviously
⑤ Probably, most important ⑥ most significant changes

簡報時的詞彙選擇

簡報時應考量該簡報的性質及聽衆，以決定必須用正式的表現方式，還是要採用較為親切沒有距離感的口氣。請參考下表熟悉正式及非正式的字彙用語。

正式 (Formal)	非正式 (Informal)	意思
accelerate	speed up	加速
amalgamate	combine	結合
conduct	carry out	實行
consolidate	strengthen	強化
capitalize on	take advantage of	利用
collaborate	work together	合作
calculate	work out	計算
demonstrate	show	展示
dispatch	send	送
establish	set up	設立
exploit	make use of	開發利用
explore	think about	探究
formulate	think up	規劃
investigate	look into	調查
incorporate	build in	統合
penetrate	break into	打入
purchase	buy	購買
relocate	move	遷移
remunerate	pay	支付
utilize	use	利用

Week 3

| 星期日第二堂課 |

強調 (2)

There's no alternative but to save energy.

〉〉跟著崔副理一起學習用來強調意義的表現方式。

強調的表現方式
用副詞強調
我們強烈建議～。
We strongly recommend that ~.
強調別無方法
我們別無選擇，只能～。
There is no alternative but to ~.
重複同樣的詞彙
沒有人比我們更了解那點——沒有人。
Nobody knows that better than we do – nobody.

Kate 老師的重點提示

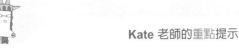

□ **確實的 accurately** exactly 的意思，to be accurate 就是「正確來說」的意思。

□ **能夠負擔 afford** 後面加不定詞 to，是「可以～、有辦法～」的意思。而在 We cannot afford the expense.（我們沒有辦法負擔費用。）這樣表達否定意味的句子裡，在 afford 後面加上名詞即可。

□ **重要，是問題 matter** 主要用在疑問句或是否定句裡，意思是「重要、成為問題」，比方說 It matters to me.（對我來說很重要。）

□ **非常，很 much** 表示「量」或「程度」很大，通常會跟 so, too, very 一起使用，反義詞是 little。

□ **實行 carry out** 意思是「著手進行某事、實行計畫」。

□ **預料 predict** 用來說明對日後的預想或是展望，名詞型是 prediction，意為「預言、預報」。

□ **沒有辦法更糟了 (It) couldn't be worse** 以反話的方式說明「最糟糕、非常糟糕」；相反的，最好的狀況就是 Couldn't be better。

透過問題來強調

所以，這究竟有多難？根本就是不可能。

So, just how difficult is it? Almost out of the question.

否定句—肯定句對照

是誰來做～不重要，重要的是如何～。

It doesn't matter who ~. What does matter is how ~.

自問自答來強調

所以，問題是什麼？問題就是～。

So, what is the problem? The problem is ~.

Key Expressions 6

除了使用「我強烈主張～」或「～是最重要的」這樣直接地表達，也可以用其他不同的方式來強調自己要傳遞的信息。下面就讓我們看看有哪些方法可以引起聽衆的共鳴。

MP3 25

01 We strongly recommend that customer-relationship skills should be taught.

我們強烈建議顧客關係技巧應該被教導。

在做簡報時想要強調某個特定信息時，可在主要的動詞之前搭配適當的副詞來加強語氣。例如 strongly recommend、solemnly promise、firmly believe 這幾個副詞與動詞就經常搭配使用。

使用強調的副詞

- We solemnly promise that this project will succeed.
  我們鄭重地保證這個計畫一定會成功。
- We firmly believe that our advertising budget should be increased.
  我們堅信我們的廣告預算應該要增加。

02 Our job rating has been much, much better than we ever expected.

我們的工作評價比原本預期的好太多了。

在簡報時可以重複想要強調的字以強化信息的意義。重複的技巧很多樣，如下面幾個例句所示。

重複使用詞彙來強調

- It really is very, very difficult to predict the political situation in the Middle East.
  中東的政治情勢實在是太難預料了。
- It's always far, far easier to make a plan than it is to carry it out.
  制定計畫總是遠比實行計畫容易。
- Nobody knows that better than we do – nobody.
  沒有人比我們更了解那點——沒有人。
- Everybody makes mistakes – everybody.
  每個人都會犯錯——每個人。

在句子最後重複一次帶有重要意義的單字也是常用的強調方式。

》還有這樣的表現方式

We didn't accept their offer. We didn't accept their offer because their final price was higher than we expected.
我們沒有接受他們的報價。我們沒有接受他們的報價因為他們最後的價錢比我們預期的高。

可以重複帶有重要信息的整個句子來做強調。

03 It doesn't matter who controls the project. What does matter is how to control it.

誰來掌控專案並不重要，重要的是如何掌控。

也可以用否定與肯定句對照來強調，這種方式可以讓後面的肯定句更有力道。後一句用 what 開始，句子會很有效果。

對照強調

- It does not concern me how fast a person can write. What does concern me is how accurately a person can write.
  我不在乎一個人能寫多快，我在乎的是他能寫得多正確。
- Investing in China does not interest me. What does interest me is finding a business partner in China.
  在中國投資我沒有興趣，我有興趣的是在中國找到一個生意夥伴。
- We have been able to fix the product if it is out of order. What we haven't been able to do is (to) exchange it for a new one.
  目前我們可以做的是修理故障產品，我們沒有辦法做到的是更換一個新的。
- We are in a good position to recommend the person you are looking for. What we are not in a position to do is (to) ask the person to work for you.
  我們有足夠的立場推薦你想要的人，但是我們沒有立場要這個人為你工作。

So, what is the problem? The problem is how we are going to finance the project.

所以，問題是什麼？問題是我們要如何資助這個專案。

這是透過問題來強調的語法。丟出問題可以先抓住聽衆的注意力，之後再丟出答案就是更有效果的強調方式。

透過問題來強調 ①

- What's our main objective? Our main objective is to build a new factory.
  我們的主要目標是什麼？我們的主要目標就是建立一個新工廠。
- And what is the result? The result is a total failure.
  而結果是什麼？結果就是完全的失敗。
- So, what is the point? The point is we can't expect too much too soon.
  所以，重點是什麼？重點就是我們不能在短期內有太多的期待。
- So, what is the solution? The solution is to get rid of the middle managers in order to make our decision-making process fast.
  所以，解決方案是什麼？解決方案就是去除中階管理人員以便讓我們的決策過程更快。

05 So, just how good is the situation? Couldn't be better.

所以，究竟狀況有多好？不能再好了。

下面是透過問題來強調的另外一種型態。04 是用問題來吸引聽衆的注意力，這裡則是問題裡就已經有答案。

透過問題來強調 ②

- So, just how bad is the situation? Couldn't be worse.
  所以，究竟狀況有多糟？不能再糟了。
- So, just how difficult is it? Almost out of the question.
  所以，這究竟有多難？根本就是不可能。
- So, just how competitive are we? Invincible.
  所以，究竟我們的競爭力如何？根本無敵。
- So, how good are our sales figures? Couldn't be better.
  所以，我們的銷售數字如何？好到不能再好。
- So, how much market share does the new product maintain? A fantastic amount.
  所以，新產品維持了多少市占率？一個驚人的數字。

There is no alternative but to increase production by 100%.

我們別無選擇，只能讓產量增加 100%。

最後還可以用 There is no alternative but to ~（除~之外，沒有別的方法）這樣的方式來強調意見。

強調別無他法

- There is no alternative but to relocate our headquarters.
  我們別無選擇，只能搬移總部。
- There is no alternative but to cut costs.
  我們別無選擇，只能減少成本。
- There is no alternative but to save energy.
  我們別無選擇，只能節約能源。

›› 還有這樣的表現方式

There is no way but to give it one more try.
我們沒有別的方法，只能再試一次。

There is no choice but to develop a new product to step up our competitiveness in the marketplace.
我們別無選擇，只能開發新產品來增加我們的市場競爭力。

隨堂測驗 A

請用提示的單字完成句子。

1 我們堅信我們的廣告預算應該要增加。
(believe / firmly / that / we)

→ ______________ our advertising budget should be increased.

2 我們的工作評價比原本預期的好太多了。
(much / ever / than / better / we / expected / much)

→ Our job rating has been ______________

3 而結果是什麼？結果就是完全的失敗。
(what / the / and / result / is)

→ ______________ The result is a total failure.

4 誰來掌控專案並不重要，重要的是如何掌控。
(does / what / to / is / how / matter)

→ It doesn't matter who controls the project.

______________ control it.

5 所以，這究竟有多難？根本就是不可能。
(difficult / is / so / how / just / it)

→ ______________ Almost out of the question.

6 我們別無選擇，只能減少成本。
(but / there / to / no / alternative / is)

→ ______________ cut costs.

隨堂測驗 B

請參考中文提示完成簡報內容。

線上事業要賺到利潤是**非常非常困難的**，因為市場已經飽和了。我們為了線上用戶創設的「現在網路」從開始就一直在賠錢。

It really is ①________ ________ ________ to make a profit in an online business because the market is already saturated. We have been losing money ever since we started Now Net for online users.

所以，狀況究竟有多糟？**不能再糟了**。如果是這樣，有**任何機會**可以扭轉劣勢嗎？有的。我們需要耐心。

So, just how bad is the situation? ②________ ________ ________. If so, is there ③________ ________ to turn the tide? Yes, there is. We need patience.

*turn the tide：扭轉劣勢

我想要**說**的是，我們不能在短期之內期待太多。我**直到**最近才**了解**這有多麼重要。沒有人在開創事業的第一年或第二年就賺錢——**沒有人**。

What I'm trying ④________ ________ is that we can't expect too much too soon. I didn't ⑤________ this was so important ⑥________ recently. Nobody earns money during their first and second years in business — ⑦________.

我們已經等了兩年。何不再等一年？

We have already waited two years. Why not wait one more year?

如果能讓我**根據**兩年前發表過的商業計畫來預估銷售數字，我們在第三年就會達到損益平衡。

If you allow me to talk about our projected sales figures ⑧________ ________ the business plan presented two years ago, we will reach the break-even point at year three.

我們需要的是各位的耐心與理解。

⑨________ ________ ________ is your patience and understanding.

隨堂測驗 A

1 We firmly believe that 2 much, much better than we ever expected
3 And what is the result? 4 What does matter is how to
5 So, just how difficult is it? 6 There is no alternative but to

隨堂測驗 B

① very, very difficult ② Couldn't be worse ③ any chance[opportunity]
④ to say ⑤ realize ⑥ until ⑦ nobody ⑧ based on ⑨ What we need

Bonus

主動和被動表現方式的語感差異

主動 (active) 的表現方式比被動 (passive) 來的不正式而且隨性。

主動的表現方式	被動的表現方式
I think ~ 我認為～	It is thought ~ 一般認為～
The manager has said ~ 經理說～	It has been said ~ 有人說～
The section chief called a meeting. 部門主任召開了一場會議。	A meeting was called. 有一場會議被召開。
I will prepare this report. 我會準備報告。	This report will be prepared. 這個報告會準備好。
We tested each person. 我們測試了每個人。	Each person was tested. 每個人都被測試了。
They carried out the first research. 他們進行了第一次研究。	The first research was carried out. 第一次研究被進行了。
Everybody knows that ~ 每個人都知道～	It is a well-known fact that ~ 這是一個衆所周知的事實～
A lot of people don't realize that ~ 很多人不知道～	It is a little known fact that ~ 這是一個不太為人所知的事實～
People often make the mistake of thinking ~ 人們常錯以為～	It is a common misconception that ~ 這是一個常發生的誤解～
We can't be sure whether we can ~ 我們不確定是否可以～	It is debatable whether ~ 是否～是有爭議的
We don't expect ~ 我們並不期待～	It is doubtful whether ~ 是否～是令人懷疑的

Week 3 複習時間

A. 使用下面的單字完成句子。

worse	bad	important	not	addition
basis	nobody	what	especially	

1 This plan has been created on the __________ of five years of market research.
這個計畫是根據五年的市場調查所訂出來的。

2 In __________, we don't have any funds available.
此外，我們沒有可以使用的資金。

3 What is __________ __________ is prolonging the period of the project.
尤其重要的是要延長專案的時間。

4 Nobody knows that better than we do — __________.
沒有人比我們更了解那點——沒有人。

5 So, just how __________ is the situation? Couldn't be __________.
所以，狀況有多糟？不能再糟了。

6 Investing in China does __________ interest me. __________ does interest me is finding a business partner in China.
在中國投資我沒有興趣，我有興趣的是在中國找到一個生意夥伴。

B. 使用提示句完成下列句子。

1 我們產品跟其他產品的不同就在於它易於使用的設計概念。

Hint What makes A distinguishable from B

→ ______________________________

2 產量的增加與獎勵有密切的關係。

Hint be closely related to

→ ______________________________

3 我們對沒有趕上期限深感遺憾。

Hint deeply regret / meet the deadline

→ ______________________________

4 我們別無選擇，只能遷移總部。

Hint There is no alternative but to ~

→ ______________________________

5 我們會增加預算，更明確地說，就是員工福利的錢。

Hint to be more specific

→ ______________________________

6 我直到媒體報導才了解這有多麼重要。

Hint not realize ~ until …

→ ______________________________

C. 根據提示完成下面簡報的空格。

1

The importance of taking good care of our customers can't ________ ________ ________ ________. Without them, we simply cannot exist. However, our reputation in terms of managing our customers is not ________ ________. This fact has been corroborated by a recent survey on the customer satisfaction ratings of our services. ________ ________ the survey, we were rated poorly, earning somewhere from six to seven on a scale of ten.

照顧好客戶的重要性再怎麼強調也不為過，沒有客戶，我們就沒有辦法生存。然而，我們在客戶管理這方面的聲譽不是那麼令人鼓舞。最近一項有關客戶滿意度的調查已經證實了這個事實。依據該調查，我們被評價為不良，滿分十分只得到六到七分。

2

So, what is the problem? ________ ________ ________ that we tend to consider our customers as a nuisance although we know that customer relationships are at the heart of our business.

On ________ ________ ________, an unfortunate accident took place last month. That is, one of our customers sued us for ignoring his repeated requests to refund his money. If we made a mistake, we will pay for it. We know that everybody can make a mistake — ________. ________ we can't afford to do, however, is to make the same mistake again.

所以，問題是什麼？問題就是，我們明明知道客戶關係是我們事業的核心，卻有把客戶當作麻煩的傾向。

更重要的是，上個月發生了一個不幸的意外，那就是，有一個客戶控告我們無視他多次要求退款的請求。如果我們犯了錯，就要付出代價。我們知道每一個人都會犯錯──每一個人。然而，我們不能承擔的是再犯同樣的錯誤。

3

________ ________ ________ is how to improve our relationships with our customers. Here we are talking about customers who pay our wages. I mean that we earn our bread because of them. And the quality and quantity of our bread is ________ ________ ________ the service we give to our customers. So, ________ are we going to solve this problem? Here are some tips. (...)

I am sure we can ________ ________ ________, i.e., improve our customer services, if we treat them like our friends or family members.

現在的問題是，我們該如何改善與客戶的關係。我們在這兒討論的可是付我們薪水的客戶。我的意思是，我們有麵包是因為他們，而我們麵包的質跟量與我們提供給客戶的服務有密切的關係。所以，我們該如何改善這個問題？下面是幾個妙招。(……)
我相信我們可以達成目標，也就是改善我們的客服，只要我們能把他們當作自己的朋友或家人來對待。

Answers

A 1 basis 2 addition 3 especially important 4 nobody 5 bad / worse 6 not / What

B 1 What makes our product distinguishable from others is its user-friendly design concept.
2 Increased production is closely related to incentives.
3 We deeply regret that we did not meet the deadline.
4 There is no alternative but to relocate our headquarters.
5 We will increase our budget, to be more specific, the money for the welfare of our employees.
6 I didn't realize this was so important until the media reported on it.

C 1 be emphasized too much / very encouraging / According to
2 The problem is / top of that / everybody / What
3 The issue here / closely related to / how / reach our goal

Week 4

結束篇

星期六第一堂課 總結重點

星期六第二堂課 結束簡報

星期日第一堂課 接受問題

星期日第二堂課 處理問題

複習時間

Week

4

總結重點

Let me sum up the main points again.

| 星期六第一堂課 |

〉〉在這堂課裡，讓我們一起跟著崔副理來看看要如何將簡報內容重新整理並做總結。

開始總結之前

讓我重新總結一下重點。

Let me sum up the main points again.

請牢記以下的建議。

Please keep the following suggestions in mind.

如各位所見，有幾個非常好的理由。

As you can see, there are some very good reasons.

我相信可以從這當中學到的教訓是很清楚明白的。

I am sure the lessons to be learned from this are evident.

Kate 老師的重點提示

- □ **總 結** **summarize / sum up** It may be summarized as follows 就是「可以總結如下」之意。
- □ **重溫** **go over** 除了「超過」的意思之外，也有「複習、重溫」的含義。另，也可以用 repeat 來替換。
- □ **複習要點** **recap** 跟 sum up 同義，是 recapitulate 的口語型態，名詞與動詞型相同。
- □ **簡述** **in brief,** 要簡述前面說過的內容時，可以在句子開頭加上這個片語或是 to sum up, / in short,。
- □ **牢 記** **keep ~ in mind** 用於傳達某些內容希望對方記住時，也可以說 Remember that ~。
- □ **造成～結果** **result in** 也可以用 turn out 來表達。
- □ **重 點** **main point / essential point** 用於當你說要提「重點」時，也就是將要整理簡報的「核心」時。

開始總結

用分詞句來做總結

總結我剛剛所做的簡報，～。

Summarizing what I have been presenting, ~.

用副詞句來做總結

簡而言之，不佳的客服將會～。

In short, poor customer service will ~.

Key Expressions 6

在說完所有的簡報內容之後，必須將核心重點做出總結整理。發表者是否能簡單明瞭地傳達要點，決定了該簡報能否達成目的。

MP3 28

01 Let me sum up the main points again.

讓我重新總結一下重點。

講完所有簡報的內容之後，可以用上面這個句子來開始進行最後的總結。這種方式對內容很多的簡報來說非常自然。

總結開始前 ①

- Let me sum up the key points again.
  讓我重新總結一下要點。
- Let me sum up the main issues.
  讓我總結一下主要的問題。
- Let me sum up the main points of my presentation.
  讓我總結一下我簡報的重點。

›› 還有這樣的表現方式

Here is a summary of the main points.
這些是重點的總結。

Let me give you a recap of how we did versus how we projected we would do.
讓我為各位回顧一下我們所做的與原本預期會做的。

I'd like to go over that again.
我想重複一次那點。

02 Please keep the following suggestions in mind.

請牢記以下的建議。

開始總結前，可以用請託的方式來集中聽衆的注意力。

總結開始前 ②

- Please keep the following recommendations in mind.
  請牢記以下的建議。
- Please bear the following points in mind.
  請牢記以下幾點。
- Please bear the following possibilities in mind.
  請牢記以下的可能性。

›› 還有這樣的表現方式

The main points of my advertising strategy **are as follows**.
我的廣告策略重點如下。

The key points of my conclusion **are as follows**.
我結論的要點如下。

My recommendations **are as follows**.
我的建議如下。

03 Let me point out the messages to be drawn from this.

讓我指出從這所得出的訊息。

做總結時常用帶有總結意涵的 message / lesson / implications / significance 等字。

總結開始前 ③

- Let me talk about the implications of this.
  讓我談談這意味著什麼。
- Let me recap the essential points.
  讓我重述一下要點。
- Let me repeat that we did not understand the significance of the personal-technology market.
  讓我重申一下，我們並不了解個人科技市場的重要性。

›› 還有這樣的表現方式

I am sure **the lessons** to be learned from this are evident.
我相信可以從這當中學到的教訓是很清楚明白的。

這個句子裡的 evident 也可以用 clear 或 obvious 來替換。

Summarizing what I have been talking about, we have no choice but to withdraw from the market.

總結我剛剛所說的，我們沒有選擇，只能撤出市場。

如果想要用一個句子來作結，可以用 summarizing 的分詞來開始句子。

用分詞句來總結

- Summarizing what I have been presenting, expansion would be difficult.
  總結我剛剛所做的簡報，擴張會很困難。

- Summarizing my points, we need to develop a training program.
  總結我的觀點，我們需要制訂一個培訓計畫。

- Summarizing what we have been discussing, we need to introduce TQM to our factories.
  總結我們剛剛所做的討論，我們工廠需要採行全面品質管理。

TQM 就是 Total Quality Management（全面品質管理）。

05 In short, poor customer service will result in a slowdown in sales.

簡而言之，不佳的客服會造成銷售衰退。

欲以一個句子來做總結時，開頭可以用帶有「總結來說」意味的副詞片語。

用副詞句來總結

- In short, the introduction of the 6 Sigma Movement led to a 10% increase in productivity.
  簡而言之，採行六標準差管理使得產能增加了 10%。
- In short, anyone can become the boss of one's own business.
  簡而言之，任何人都可以成為自己事業的老闆。
- In short, according to the market research, sales of this product have increased.
  簡而言之，根據市場調查，這項產品的銷售已經增加。

›› 還有這樣的表現方式

Briefly, we can't take any chances.
簡單來說，我們不能冒任何風險。

To sum up, this is one of the most efficient approaches to our problem.
總而言之，這是解決我們問題最有效的方法之一。

To put it briefly, sales have increased tenfold.
簡單地說，銷售量增加了十倍。

06 As you can see, there are some very good reasons.

如各位所見，有幾個非常好的理由。

以「As ＋ 主詞 ＋ 動詞」之句型開頭，在句子的一開始就點出「如剛剛所說」、「如各位所見」之類的話，聽衆就會知道接下來的內容將會是總結。

用副詞句來總結

- As we have been discussing so far, there are some vital signs.
  如我們到目前所討論的，有幾個極重要的跡象。
- As we have seen, there are some suggestions.
  如我們所看到的，有幾個建議。
- As you can see, there have been some concerns.
  如各位所見，一直以來都有一些疑慮。
- As we have been discussing, we need to come up with some proper methods.
  如我們剛剛所討論的，我們必須想出一些適當的辦法。

隨堂測驗 A

請用提示的單字完成句子。

1 讓我重新總結一下重點。
(sum / the / points / me / let / up / main)

→ ______________________________ again.

2 總結我剛剛所做的簡報，擴張會很困難。
(what / been / have / I / summarizing / presenting)

→ ______________________________, expansion would be difficult.

3 簡而言之，不佳的客服會造成銷售衰退。
(service / in / poor / short / customer)

→ ______________________________ will result in a slowdown in sales.

4 從這當中學到的教訓是很清楚明白的。
(learned / this / the / to / lessons / be / from)

→ ______________________________ are evident.

5 如我們所看到的，有幾個原因。
(seen / as / have / we)

→ ______________________________, there are several reasons.

6 請牢記以下的建議。
(suggestions / mind / keep / in / the / following)

→ Please ______________________________.

隨堂測驗 B

請參考中文提示完成簡報內容。

MP3 29

1

這邊是幾個要讓 X 計畫成功之要點的**總結**。第一是產品品質，第二是客戶服務與客戶滿意度，第三是經銷通路的管道。

Here is ________ ________ ________ the keys to success for Product X. One — product quality. Two — customer service and customer satisfaction. Three — access to distribution channels.

2

讓我**總結一下**要點。首先，我們必須將第一年的虧損控制在十萬美金之內，第二，我們在第二年要能掌握能直接賣給客戶的經銷通路，最後，我們在第三年必須獲利。

Let ________ ________ ________ the essential points. First, we have to limit losses in year one to less than $100,000. Second, we should secure direct distribution channels to our customers in year two. Lastly, we must make a profit in year three.

3

總結我們到目前所討論的，管理團隊對這個計畫的成功而言是不可或缺的，而且必須在行銷管理、財務與服務開發上有很強的基礎。

________ ________ we have been talking about so far, the management team is integral to the success of this project and must have a strong foundation in marketing management, finance, and services development.

4

簡而言之，我們相信現在是開始新創投事業的好時機。

In ________, we believe the timing is right for starting this new venture business.

5

如各位所見，一直以來都有**一些疑慮**。原油價格不斷飆升、美國政府維持著美金弱勢的政策，而我們的純益已經大減至三百萬美金。

________ ________ ________, there have been ________ ________. Crude oil prices are soaring. The US government is maintaining a weak dollar policy. And our net profits have been drastically reduced to $3 million.

6

請牢記**以下的建議**。我們需要知道消費者擁有些什麼樣的資訊，有了這樣的資訊我們才容易提出升級的建議。

Please keep ________ ________ ________ in mind. We need information about what consumers own. That information makes it easy for us to offer upgrade suggestions.

Bonus

商業上會用到的縮寫 (abbreviation)

- **CEO** (Chief Executive Officer) 執行長
- **IMF** (International Monetary Fund) 國際貨幣基金
- **AGM** (Annual General Meeting) 年度股東大會
- **GDP** (Gross Domestic Product) 國內生產毛額
- **GNI** (Gross National Income) 國民所得淨額
- **NAFTA** (North American Free Trade Agreement) 北美自由貿易協定
- **GATT** (General Agreement on Trade and Tariffs) 關稅暨貿易總協定
- **CPI** (Consumer Price Index) 消費者物價指數
- **VAT** (Value Added Tax) 增值稅
- **R&D** (Research and Development) 研究開發
- **RPM** (Retail Price Maintenance) 維持轉售價格（製造業公司將自己的產品定在一個價位，讓代理商無法隨意降價的一種系統）。
- **PR** (Public Relations) 公關
- **MD** (Managing Director) 董事總經理（CEO 的英式用法）
- **CV** (Curriculum Vitae) 履歷
- **MBO** (Management by Objectives) 目標管理（用目標達成與否來評價工作表現的一種管理系統）
- **TQM** (Total Quality Management) 全面品質管理（將產品品質與服務看為第一優先的管理系統）

隨堂測驗 A

1 Let me sum up the main points 2 Summarizing what I have been presenting
3 In short, poor customer service 4 The lessons to be learned from this
5 As we have seen 6 keep the following suggestions in mind

隨堂測驗 B

1 a summary of 2 me sum up 3 Summarizing what 4 short
5 As you see / some concerns 6 the following suggestions

Week

4

| 星期六第二堂課 |

結束簡報

That concludes my presentation.

〉〉跟著崔副理一起來看看結束簡報的表現方式。

結束簡報

我的簡報到此結束。

That concludes my presentation.

在做最終結論前

在我結束之前，讓我重複一下重點。

Before I stop, let me just repeat the main points.

最後我想說，我們必須～。

I'd like to finish by saying that we have to ~.

Kate 老師的重點提示

□ **下結論** conclude 簡報結束欲做總結時，可以用具有「總之、結論就是」這類含義的語詞來開頭，如 In conclusion 或是 To conclude。

□ **結束，作結** end / close / finish「將以說～來做結束」的說法就是 I'd like to end[finish] by saying ~。

□ **網羅、包含一切** cover 這個字的意思是「到某個範圍『為止』」，或是「『包含』某個領域」。做簡報時可以用 That covers my presentation 來表明「簡報到此為止」。

□ **強調** stress / emphasize 簡報結束的同時想要再次做強調時，可以說 Let me stress[emphasize] that ~。

□ **也就是說、即** that is to say 也可以說 In other words 或是 To put it another way。

□ **參與、出席** participate 可以用 Thank you for your participation. 來感謝出席的聽眾。

做結論

總之，我們需要的是～。

In conclusion, what we need is ~.

這就是我這次簡報想要說的。

That's what this presentation is all about.

道感謝

感謝各位的聆聽。

Thank you for listening.

Key Expressions 6

在做簡報之結論時，為了讓自己的主張和見解能充分被表達，可以再一次用強調來做出明確的總結。以下是可以運用的表達方式。

01 That concludes my presentation.

我的簡報到此結束。

一般可以直接用這句話來結束簡報。若想要給人較不正式的隨性感，也可以用 talk 或是 the formal part of my talk 來取代 presentation。

結束簡報

- That covers all that I wanted to say today.
  以上就是我今天想要說的。
- That completes my presentation.
  我的簡報到此為止。
- That ends my talk.
  我的發表到此為止。

〉〉還有這樣的表現方式

That brings us to the end of my presentation.
我的簡報到此結束。

02 Before I stop, let me just repeat the main points of my talk.

在我結束之前，讓我重複一次我所講的重點。

作結的時候除了可以直接表明 That's all that I want to say today（以上是我今天想要講的內容）之外，用重複簡報重點來作結也是不錯的方式。

用重複重點來作結 ①

- Before I finish, let me stress why we must withdraw from the overseas market.
  在我結束之前，讓我再次強調我們為何需要撤出海外市場。
- Before I end, let me point one more time to the importance of restructuring.
  在我結束之前，讓我再一次點出組織重整的重要性。
- Before I close, let me emphasize the importance of outsourcing to save money.
  在我結束之前，讓我強調外包以節省費用的重要性。

›› 還有這樣的表現方式

The main benefits of the new design **hardly need to be emphasized**.
新設計的好處幾乎不需要再多加強調。

There is not a shadow of doubt in my mind that we can increase production by 50%.
我心中對增加 50% 產量的可能性沒有任何一絲懷疑。

03 I'd like to end by emphasizing the importance of making a new logo.

最後我想再次強調製作新商標的重要性。

在做簡報時必須能將主要論點用一句話表達出來，並在做結論時再強調一次這個論點，讓聽衆留下更深刻的印象。

用重複重點來作結 ②

- I'd like to end with the idea that we need to continue putting emphasis on international operations.
  最後我想再次提醒，我們必須持續將重點放在國際事業營運上。

- I'd like to conclude by repeating that we need to refocus on our online business.
  最後我要重申，我們需要重新聚焦在我們的線上事業。

- I'd like to leave you with the idea that we need to set up new computer system.
  最後我想再次提醒各位，我們需要設置新的電腦系統。

- I'd like to finish by saying that we have to get bank loans to finance the overseas project.
  最後我想說，我們必須跟銀行貸款來資助海外計畫。

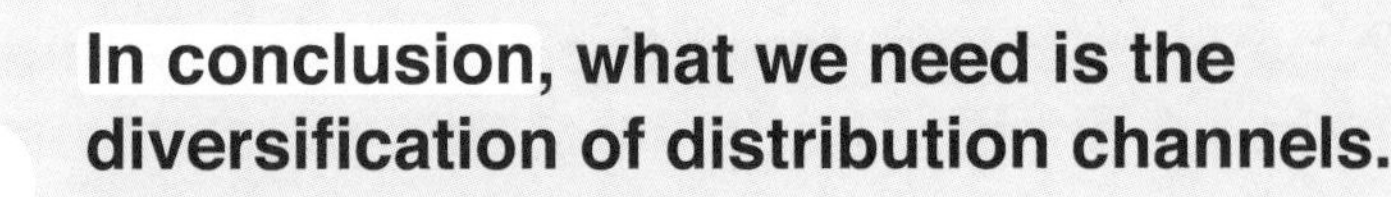

04 In conclusion, what we need is the diversification of distribution channels.

結論就是，我們需要讓經銷通路更多元化。

即使不用動詞 end / complete / finish 來宣告「結束」，只要提到 conclusion，聽衆就能知道你的簡報即將結束。如果有兩個結論可說 There are two conclusions，而簡報裡有兩個建議則可說 There are two recommendations。

做結論

- In conclusion, what we need is to lower our price.
  結論就是，我們需要降低價格。
- In conclusion, I think we need to penetrate the target market.
  結論就是，我認為我們需要打入目標市場。
- In conclusion, we can gain a lot by employing that program.
  結論就是，我們可以經由採用該方案獲取很多好處。

›› 還有這樣的表現方式

To conclude, we need to revise our brand to satisfy the sensibilities of young people.
結論就是，我們需要修正我們的品牌以滿足年輕人敏銳的感覺。

05 We have to close down the plants that are not making a profit. That's what this presentation is all about.

我們必須關閉不賺錢的工廠。這就是我簡報所要說的。

還有一種作結方式與前面提到的略為不同，就是先簡單的講出結論，再向聽衆表示這是簡報的重點。

直接說出結論

- We have to reduce the consumption of fossil fuels. That's what this presentation is all about.

  我們需要減少石油燃料的使用。這就是我簡報所要說的。

›› 還有這樣的表現方式

So, what does all this mean? That is to say, we should take the long-term benefits into consideration.
所以，這代表什麼意思？這就是說，我們需要考慮到長遠的利益。

So, what does all this mean? That is to say, if we do not protect our technology, we will soon be out of business.
所以，這代表什麼意思？這就是說，如果不保護好我們的技術，我們很快就會關門大吉。

So, what does all this mean? That is to say, we have to close down the plants that are not making a profit.
所以，這代表什麼意思？這就是說，我們需要關閉不賺錢的工廠。

也可以用修飾性的問題來作結：先用問題來抓住聽衆的注意，接著講出答案，在再次強調自己主張的同時結束簡報。

Thank you for listening (to my presentation).

感謝各位的聆聽（我的簡報）。

結束簡報時不要忘記感謝聽眾。如果在表示感謝之後再加上 I hope you have gained an insight into ~（希望各位對～有了更深的了解），會讓你的簡報感覺更具水準。

表示感謝

- Thank you for your attention.
  感謝各位的專注。
- Thank you for being such a good audience.
  感謝各位專注聆聽。
- Thank you for being with us this morning.
  感謝各位今天早上的參與。
- Thank you all for attending.
  感謝大家的參與。
- Thanks for your participation.
  感謝各位的參與。
- I'd like to thank Mr. Smith for coming over from Canada.
  我要感謝史密斯先生特別從加拿大前來。

隨堂測驗 A

請用提示的單字完成句子。

1 我的簡報到此結束。
(presentation / that / my / concludes)

→ ______________________________

2 在我結束之前，讓我重複一次我所講的重點。
(repeat / me / points / the / let / main / just)

→ Before I stop, ______________________________ of my talk.

3 最後我想再次強調製作新商標的重要性。
(end / to / emphasizing / I'd / like / by)

→ ______________________________ the importance of making a new logo.

4 結論就是，我認為我們需要打入目標市場。
(think / to / in / conclusion / I / have / we)

→ ______________________________ penetrate the target market.

5 我們必須關閉不賺錢的工廠。這就是我簡報所要說的。
(this / what / That's / presentation / about / is / all)

→ We have to close down the plants that are not making a profit.
______________________________.

6 感謝各位的聆聽。
(thank / for / you / listening)

→ ______________________________

B

請參考中文提示完成簡報內容。

MP3 31

1

現在該是**結束**我今天**簡報**的時候了。所以，如同我們到目前所討論的，我們不能再等下去了。我們必須進行組織重整以維持市場競爭力。如何做呢？我今天已經給了各位**答案**。

Now, it is time to ①________ ________ ________ today. So, as we have discussed so far, we cannot afford to wait any longer. We have to restructure to remain competitive in the market. How? I gave you ②________ ________ today.

簡而言之，我們可以用重整事業結構、關閉不賺錢的海外工廠，以及實行提前退休計畫來達成目標。

To ③________ ________, we can achieve our goal by reorganizing our business structure, by shutting down unprofitable overseas factories, and by implementing an early retirement plan.

在我結束**之前**，我想**感謝**各位的參與。我很樂意回答各位任何問題。

④________ I finish, I'd like to ⑤________ ________ ________ your participation. I'd be glad to answer any questions you might have.

2

所以，在我**結束**之前，讓我**重述**一次新竹的優點。首先，它的地理位置方便：新竹四通八達。第二，人力資源豐富：找到符合資格的人力一點也不難。

So, before I ①________, let me just ②________ ________ the key benefits of Hsinchu. Firstly, its convenient location: you can go anywhere from Hsinchu. Secondly, human resources: you will have no problem in recruiting well-qualified workers.

請讓我再次**強調**，您不需要花費寶貴的時間尋找未來投資的地點。您要的答案就是新竹。

Let me once again ③________, please, that you do not have to spend your precious time looking for a site for your future investment. The answer is Hsinchu.

感謝您的**聆聽**。我相信各位現在有很多問題，我會很樂意回答。

Thank you for ④________. Now, I am sure you have lots of questions, and I will be happy to take them.

Bonus

與聽眾建立融洽的關係 (1)

與聽衆建立融洽關係，即所謂的“rapport”，是成功簡報的必要條件之一。這樣的 rapport 在簡報的一開始就要建立，為此簡報者必須注意兩件事：視線交流 (eye contact) 與聽衆參與 (audience participation)。如果有做到這兩點，這個簡報就可以說已經成功了 60%。

*rapport：用來形容兩個人之間出現互信關係的心理學用語。

- **視線交流**：在傳統東方文化的禮教中，直視對方眼睛是不禮貌的。但是在做簡報的時候，如果眼睛一直往下看，或是迴避聽衆視線的話，會讓人誤會你沒有自信，也很難得到聽衆的信賴。所以，進行簡報的時候要常常看著聽衆的眼睛。如果聽衆很多，就隨意地挑選幾個人做視線交流。

- **聽衆參與**：簡報過程中盡量接受聽衆的問題，讓聽衆能積極的參與，這樣才不會變成一言堂式的簡報，而是可以跟聽衆產生共鳴的簡報。

隨堂測驗 A

1 That concludes my presentation. 2 let me just repeat the main points
3 I'd like to end by emphasizing 4 In conclusion, I think we have to
5 That's what this presentation is all about. 6 Thank you for listening.

隨堂測驗 B

1 ① conclude[end / complete] my presentation ② an answer ③ sum up ④ Before ⑤ thank you for
2 ① finish[stop / end / close] ② go over ③ emphasize[stress] ④ listening

Week 4

接受問題

Are there any questions?

| 星期日第一堂課 |

〉〉請看接受聽衆問題並且回答時可以用哪些表達方式！

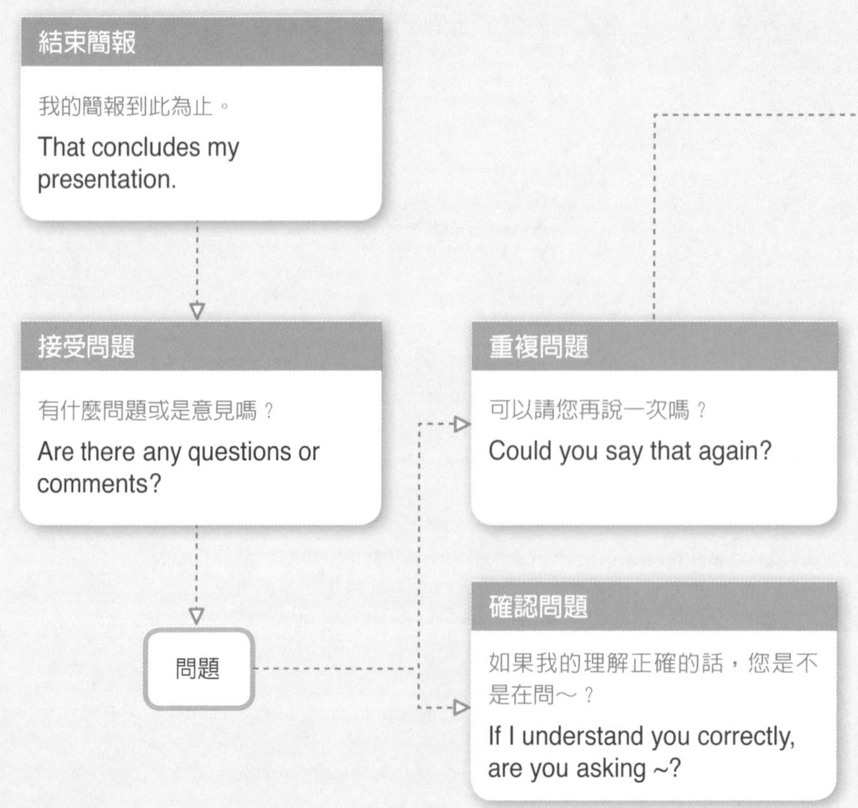

結束簡報
我的簡報到此為止。
That concludes my presentation.
接受問題
有什麼問題或是意見嗎？
Are there any questions or comments?
問題
重複問題
可以請您再說一次嗎？
Could you say that again?
確認問題
如果我的理解正確的話，您是不是在問～？
If I understand you correctly, are you asking ~?

- □ **提問** **ask a question**「問某人問題」是 ask + 人 + a question 或是 ask a question of + 人，要注意文法排列。
- □ **回答問題** **answer a question** 表示「回答」的動詞還有 reply、respond。
- □ **了解** **understand/see** 這兩個動詞的意思是「了解」，see 是較為口語的用法。
- □ **不確定～** **I'm not sure ~** 可用這個句型來表明不是很了解對方的問題，例如 I'm not sure what you are getting at.（我不是很確定你想說什麼）。
- □ **錯過** **miss** 除了可以形容錯過火車等等之外，miss 也可以用於形容不理解講話內容，相反詞是 catch（抓到、理解）。
- □ **評價、意見、見解** **comment** 簡報結束問聽衆意見時，可以說 Are there any questions or comments?（有任何問題或是意見嗎？）
- □ **不相關的、無關的** **not relevant** 當有人問到與簡報內容無關的問題時，可以說 Your question is not relevant.（你的問題並不相干）。

回答
評價問題
這是個非常好的問題。
That's a very good question.
這恐怕是個相當不好回答的問題。
I am afraid that is a rather difficult question.
我認為這個問題並不相干。
I think that question is not relevant.
詢問對回答的滿意程度
這樣有回答到您的問題嗎？
Does that answer your question?
換到下一個問題
我們可以繼續嗎？
May we move on?

Key Expressions 6

簡報後的問答時間是可以進一步增進聽眾理解的好機會，所以相當的重要。這堂課要學的是接受提問、確認問題並回答，以及如何再接續到下一個問題的表達方式。

MP3 32

01 Are there any questions or comments?

有什麼問題或意見嗎？

先問聽眾有沒有問題，通常有問題的聽眾會說 I have a question. 然後要求提問。這時簡報者可以用 Go ahead（請說）/ Please（請問）/ Certainly（當然可以）來回應。

詢問有無問題

- Are there any questions you'd like to ask?
  各位有什麼想問的問題嗎？

- Does anyone have any questions or comments?
  有人有問題或是意見嗎？

>> 還有這樣的表現方式

Now we have about ten minutes for questions and answers.
現在我們大概有十分鐘可以進行 Q&A。

Now I'd like to invite your questions and comments.
現在請各位提出問題和意見。

I would be happy to answer any questions.
我很樂意回答任何問題。

02 That's a very good question.

這是個非常好的問題。

當觀衆提出問題時，只要不是太荒謬的問題，都可以向對方表示感謝。

對提問表示感謝

- Thank you for asking that question.
  謝謝你提出這個問題。
- I am glad you asked that.
  我很高興你問到這個。
- That's an excellent question.
  這是個非常好的問題。
- That's a good point.
  這是個好問題。

›› 還有這樣的表現方式

＊也可以用下列表現方式來評價聽衆的問題。透過這類的評語，可以爭取到一些準備回答的時間。

I am afraid that is a rather difficult question.
這恐怕是一個相當不好回答的問題。

I think that question is not relevant.
我認為這個問題並不相干。

03 If I understand you correctly, are you asking us to restructure our department?

如果我的理解正確的話，您是不是要我們重整部門？

接受提問時，若不太理解問題，可反問問題的重點以確認內容。下列是幾種方式。

反問問題的重點

- If I understand you correctly, are you saying that we could prevent these problems?
  如果我的理解正確的話，你是不是說我們可以預防這些問題？

- If I understand you correctly, did you mean to say that we should have offered a 3% increase on their basic wages?
  如果我的理解正確的話，你的意思是說我們應該把他們的底薪加個 3% 嗎？

>> 還有這樣的表現方式

I am not sure whether I understand you correctly, but did you say that we should freeze wages?
我不確定我的理解是否正確，你是說我們應該凍結薪資嗎？

I'm not sure what you're getting at.
我不是很確定你想說什麼。

04 Could you say that again?

可以請您再說一遍嗎？

當沒聽清楚對方的問題時，可以直接請對方重複一次。以下是幾種好用的說法。

請對方重複問題

- Sorry, I missed that. Could you go over that again?
  抱歉，我沒聽清楚，可以請您再說一次嗎？
- Sorry, I didn't catch that. Could you repeat it, please?
  抱歉，我沒聽懂，可以請您再說一次嗎？
- Sorry, I don't quite see what you mean. Could you explain that, please?
  抱歉，我不是很懂您的意思。可以請您解釋一下嗎？

›› 還有這樣的表現方式

I am sorry. I was not paying attention. **What was that again?**
對不起，我沒有注意聽。你剛剛說什麼？

I don't quite follow you. **What exactly do you mean?**
你說的我不是很懂。你到底是什麼意思？

05 Does that answer your question?

這樣有回答到您的問題嗎？

回答問題之後，必須跟聽眾確定對回答的滿意程度。

詢問對回答的滿意程度

- Does my answer satisfy you?
  我的回答有讓您滿意嗎？
- Does my response make sense?
  我的回答講得通吧？
- Have I made that clear?
  那一點我說的夠清楚嗎？

›› 還有這樣的表現方式

Is that clear?
清楚嗎？

Do you see what I'm getting at?
你懂我的意思嗎？

Did I answer your question?
我有回答了你的問題嗎？

06 May we move on?

我們可以繼續嗎？

回答完一個問題之後，表明可以繼續下一個問題的說法有下列幾個。

接續下一個問題

- May we continue?
  我們可以繼續嗎？
- May we go on to the next question?
  我們可以繼續下一個問題嗎？
- If there are no further questions concerning the issue of the budget, let's move on to the next question.
  如果關於預算的議題沒有進一步的問題，我們就繼續下一個問題吧。

›› 還有這樣的表現方式

＊下面是沒有其他問題時，可以用來結束問答時間並做簡報最後收尾的說法。

If there are no other questions, why don't we wrap it up here.
如果沒有其他的問題，我們就在這裡結束吧。

If there are no further questions, perhaps we should stop here.
如果沒有進一步的問題，也許我們應該到此結束。

隨堂測驗 A

請用提示的單字完成句子。

1 有人有問題或是意見嗎？
(have / comments / any / or / questions)

→ Does anyone ______________________________

2 這是個非常好的問題。
(good / a / that / question / is / very)

→ ______________________________

3 如果我的理解正確的話，您是不是要我們重整部門？
(understand / I / you / if / correctly)

→ ______________________________, are you asking us to restructure our department?

4 可以請您再說一次嗎？
(you / that / could / again / over / go)

→ ______________________________

5 這樣有回答到你的問題嗎？
(answer / that / your / does / question)

→ ______________________________

6 我們可以繼續下一個問題嗎？
(may / on / to / we / go)

→ ______________________________ the next question?

隨堂測驗 B

請參考中文提示完成簡報內容。

1

A: 我今天的簡報到此為止。**有沒有什麼問題**？
B: 我想聽聽您對土地的成本有什麼看法。
A: 這是一個**非常好的問題**。我已經預期會有這樣的問題，所以準備了一張表來說明這個地區每平方公尺的土地價格。(……)
A: 還有其他的問題嗎？如果**沒有進一步**問題，我就講到這兒。感謝各位的提問與參與。

A: That completes my presentation today. Are ① ________ ________ ________ you'd like to ask?

B: I am interested in hearing what you have to say about the cost of the land.

A: That is a ② ________ ________ ________. Anticipating that question, I have prepared a table which will show you the price of the land in this region per square meter. (...)

A: Are there any more questions? If there are ③ ________ ________ questions, I think I should stop here. Thanks for your questions and interest.

2

A: 我們應該付大學畢業生怎樣的起薪？
B: 我很**高興您問到**這個。我給您看一個表，表格中顯示了這個產業付給四年制大學畢業生的平均薪資？

A: How much should we expect to pay for a starting salary for university graduates?

B: I'm very ________ ________ ________ that. Let me show you this table, which will tell the average salary four-year college graduates receive in this industry.

3

A: 我很好奇想知道你要怎樣確保客戶的知識可以轉換成他們的智慧財產？
B: 抱歉，我**沒聽清楚**，可以請您**再**說一次嗎？

A: I am wondering how you are going to ensure the conversion of the clients' knowledge into their intellectual property?
B: Sorry, I ① ________ that. Could you say that ② ________?

4

A: 每個人都會同意解決當下問題的唯一方法就是縮編。
B: 如果**我的理解正確的話**，你是不是要我們重整部門？

A: Everybody will agree that downsizing is the only solution to the current problem.
B: If ________ ________ ________ ________, are you asking us to restructure our department?

5

A: 可以請你說明一下 2018 年的預估營收和淨利嗎？
B: 這個計畫會讓 2018 年的營收成長到一千萬美金，淨利則會達到兩百五十萬美金。這樣有**回答到你的問題嗎**？我們可以**繼續嗎**？

A: Can you tell me about the projected sales revenues and net income in 2018?
B: This plan will result in sales revenues growing to $10 million by 2018 and will generate net income of more than $2.5 million. Does that ① ________ ________ ________? May we ② ________ ________?

Bonus

與聽眾建立融洽的關係 (2)

建立 rapport 的另一個方法就是使用特定的字詞或語句。下面三種表達方式可以幫助提高與聽眾間的親密度。

1. 使用 we (all) / us (all) / our / ours

例 Basically, we know what our goal is.
(基本上，我們知道我們的目標是什麼。)
Our goal is to increase productivity.
(我們的目標就是提高產能。)

2. 使用請求認同的附加問句。

例 We all know what our vision means, don't we?
(我們都知道我們的願景代表什麼，不是嗎？)
We don't know what the market demands, do we?
(我們並不知道市場要什麼，對吧？)

3. 使用有號召力的否定疑問句。(否定疑問句有強烈的肯定意味)

例 Haven't we decided to buy the equipment?
(我們不是決定要買那些設備了嗎？)
→ 意思是大家都知道這是個已經決定了的事實。

隨堂測驗 A

1 have any questions or comments? 2 That's a very good question.
3 If I understand you correctly 4 Could you go over that again?
5 Does that answer your question? 6 May we go on to

隨堂測驗 B

1 ① there any questions ② very good question ③ no further
2 glad you asked
3 ① missed ② again
4 I understand you correctly
5 ① answer your question ② move[go] on

Week 4

| 星期日第二堂課 |

處理問題

Sorry, perhaps I did not make that quite clear.

〉〉最後，跟著崔副理一起看看處理聽眾提問時，還會遇到哪些狀況。

需迴避答案時

我恐怕沒有立場對此發表評論。

I'm afraid I am not in a position to comment on that.

我恐怕沒有這方面的資訊。

I'm afraid I don't have that information with me.

這個我一下子想不出來。

I don't know that off the top of my head.

問題脫離討論時

對不起，我看不出關聯性。

I'm sorry, but I don't see the connection.

你的問題恐怕並不相干。

I'm afraid your question is not relevant.

Kate 老師的重點提示

□ **我恐怕～ I'm afraid that ～** 這是用於委婉謙遜的表達負面內容。afraid 原指「害怕」，後面要接介系詞 of。

□ **把 ～ 說 分 明 make ～ clear** I didn't make my point clear. 意即「我沒有說得很清楚」。

□ **正如我剛剛所提的 As I mentioned earlier** 在回答問題的同時，也表示剛才已經很明確的說明過了。

□ **理解 follow** 當「理解」的意思時，常會用疑問句的方式來表達，像是 Do you follow me?（有聽懂我的意思嗎？）。follow 原指「跟隨」。

□ **直接（不必細想）地 off the top of one's head** 形容「不必細想，一下子就能說出來的」。

□ **處理 deal with** 除了有「處理」問題與議題的意思之外，也有與人或公司「做交易」的意思。

回答問題時

正如我先前說過的，我們～。
As I talked about earlier, we ~.

我想說的是～。
What I am saying is that ~.

抱歉，或許我剛才並沒有說得很清楚。
Sorry, perhaps I did not make that quite clear.

Key Expressions 6

在進行問答的過程中，有時會出現預期之外不方便回答或是完全無從答起的問題。這種時候不要慌亂，可以用以下的表現方式來解圍。

01 I'm afraid I am not in a position to comment on that.

我恐怕沒有立場對此發表評論。

下面是你覺得職務上不方便，想要迴避聽衆提問時的好用說法。

迴避問題

- I'm afraid I am not in a position to talk about that.
  我恐怕沒有立場談論這個。
- I'm afraid I don't have that information with me.
  我恐怕沒有這方面的資訊。
- I'm afraid I don't have the figures with me.
  我恐怕並沒有確切的數據。
- I'm afraid that's not my field.
  那恐怕不是我的領域。

如果真的不知道，比起 I don't know 或 I wish I knew（我希望我知道），這是一個更好的回答。

02 I don't know that off the top of my head.

這個我一下子想不出來。

當遇到對於提問不知如何回答的狀況，若隨便亂回答的話，不僅會讓人覺得沒有誠意，更有可能會危及到簡報內容的可信度，這時可以用下列的方式來延遲回答。

延遲回答

- I can't answer your question off the top of my head.
  我一下子回答不了你的問題。
- I can't comment on that off the top of my head.
  這個我一下子不知道要如何評論。

›› 還有這樣的表現方式

＊也可以直率地表示下次再回答這個問題。

Perhaps I can get back to you on that later?
這個我可以日後再回答你嗎？

Perhaps I can talk about that later?
這個我可以之後再跟你說嗎？

Perhaps I can deal with that later?
這個我可以之後再處理嗎？

另外，也可以發揮機智將問題反問發問者，或是將問題丟給其他的聽衆。例如：

- Interesting. What do you think?
  （很有趣。你們認為呢？）
- Is there anyone who could answer that question?
  （有人能夠回答這個問題嗎？）

03 Well, as I talked about earlier, we were well behind schedule on this project.

嗯，正如我先前說過的，我們在這個計畫上的進度嚴重落後。

如果聽眾問了剛剛已經回答過或是簡報中已經提到過的內容，就可以這樣回答。

說明已經說明過

- Well, as I mentioned earlier, there is an undersupplied market in Vietnam.
  嗯，正如我先前提到的，越南是一個供給不足的市場。
- Well, as I said earlier, we have problems with one of our suppliers.
  嗯，正如我先前說的，我們與一個供應商發生了問題。
- Well, as I said at the end of my presentation, the new product should be ready by this summer.
  嗯，正如我簡報最後說的，新產品應該在今年夏天就會準備好。

›› 還有這樣的表現方式

I think I answered that earlier.
這個我想我剛剛已經回答過了。

如果你覺得這個問題沒有重複提的必要，就可以用這樣簡短有效的回應。

I'm sorry, but I don't see the connection.

對不起，我看不出關聯性。

如果提問的重點跟簡報內容無關，或是與簡報內容不符合時，可以直接指出來。

指出問題不相關

- I'm sorry, but I don't see the relevance.
  對不起，我看不出有什麼關聯。

- I'm sorry, but your question is not relevant to the subject of today's presentation.
  對不起，你的問題與本日的簡報主題無關。

> 也可以用 I am afraid 來代替 I am sorry, but ...。

›› 還有這樣的表現方式

Sorry, I don't follow you.
抱歉，我不懂你的意思。

To be honest, I think that raises a different issue.
老實說，我認為那又產生了另外一個問題。

> 「老實說」除了用 to be honest 之外，也可以用 honestly、frankly speaking 或 to be frank with you。

05 Sorry, perhaps I did not make that quite clear.

抱歉，或許我剛才並沒有說得很清楚。

如果發問者不是很能理解你的回答，就表示問題出在你簡報者的身上。這時最好謙遜的表示自己說明得不夠清楚。成功簡報的最後，必須表現出這種成熟穩健與有禮貌的姿態。

為不足的回答表示歉意

- Sorry, perhaps I did not fully explain that.
  抱歉，或許我剛才並沒有解釋得很完整。

- Sorry, perhaps I did not explain fully enough to make you understand.
  抱歉，或許我剛才並沒有解釋得足以讓您了解。

- Sorry, perhaps my explanation was not good enough to make you understand.
  抱歉，或許我的解釋不夠好沒能夠讓您了解。

enough to ~ 就是「能充分～」的意思。enough 亦可用來修飾名詞，【例】We have enough cash to buy the store.（我們有足夠的現金買下那間店。）

06 Sorry, what I am saying is, let us concentrate on doing what we do best.

抱歉，我想說的是，讓我們專注於做我們最擅長的事情。

回答完問題之後，如果覺得沒有充分的回應提問者，或是覺得自己剛才的回答有所不足時，可以明確地重新整理一次回答。

整理回答時

- Sorry, what I am saying is, we need to believe in ourselves.
  抱歉，我想說的是，我們必須相信自己。
- Sorry, what I am saying is, our survival depends upon a cost-effective strategy.
  抱歉，我想說的是，我們的生存取決於一個具成本效益的策略。

›› 還有這樣的表現方式

What I meant is that we eventually blew the deal.
我的意思是，交易最終還是被我們搞砸了。

My meaning is that our commercials should aim for the end-users.
我的意思是，我們的廣告應該要針對終端使用者。

隨堂測驗 A

請用提示的單字完成句子。

1 這個我一下子想不出來。
(top / head / the / of / my / off)

→ I don't know that ______________________________.

2 我恐怕沒有立場對此發表評論。
(on / a / position / that / to / comment / in)

→ I'm afraid I am not ______________________________.

3 正如我先前說過的，我們在這個計畫上的進度嚴重落後。
(about / I / earlier / talked / as)

→ Well, ______________________________, we were well behind schedule on this project.

4 對不起，我看不出關聯性。
(the / do / connection / see / I / not)

→ I'm sorry, but ______________________________.

5 我想說的是，我們的生存取決於一個有成本效益的策略。
(saying / I / what / is / am)

→ ______________________________ our survival depends upon a cost-effective strategy.

6 抱歉，或許我剛才並沒有解釋得很完整。
(explain / I / fully / did / that / not)

→ Sorry, perhaps ______________________________.

隨堂測驗 B

請參考中文提示完成簡報內容。

A: 我的簡報到此結束，**有任何**問題**嗎**？

A: That covers all that I wanted to say today. ①________ ________ ________ questions?

B: 你認為你的企業計畫裡的重要成功要素是什麼？

B: What do you think the critical success factors are in your business project?

A: **正如我**先前**說的**，我們可以就兩個要素來說：高品質的服務與客戶滿意度。

A: Well, ②________ ________ ________ earlier, we can talk about them in terms of two elements: high quality service and customer satisfaction.

C: 有什麼證據顯示如果我們在那邊開工廠可以獲利？

C: What evidence is there that we will make a profit if we build a factory here?

A: 我認為那又產生了**另外一個問題**。我們要說的是，我們可以提供最適合的條件讓您在新竹做生意。

A: I think that raises ③________ ________ ________. What we suggest is we can provide the most suitable conditions for you to do business here in Hsinchu.

D: 可以請你多說一些你剛才提到的免稅政策嗎？

D: Could you expand on what you said about your tax exemption policies?

A: 關於這個問題，我恐怕沒有**立場回答**，因為那不是我的領域。讓我將您的問題轉問在場來幫忙的地方政府官員。(……)

A: On that subject, I'm afraid I am not in ④________ ________ ________ ________ since that is not my field. Let me ask the same question of the local government official who is here to help us out. (…)

E: 台灣的經濟狀況一點也不好。我想知道你在做企業計畫時是否有考量到這些外在因素。

E: The economic situation in Taiwan is not good at all. I was wondering whether you took these external factors into consideration when you made your business plan.

A: 事實上我有。不過或許我的解釋不夠好沒能**讓您了解**。(……)

A: In fact, I did. But perhaps my explanation was not good enough to ⑤________ ________ ________. (…)

A: 還有其他的問題嗎？**如果沒有其他的問題**，我想我的簡報就到此結束。感謝各位的問題與參與。

A: Are there any more questions? ⑥________ ________ ________ no further questions, I think I should stop here. Thanks for your questions and interest.

與聽眾建立融洽的關係 (3)

在做簡報時可以使用一些不影響簡報內容的簡單字彙讓語氣變得更溫和，以拉近與聽衆的距離。例如：

- **You know**, over the past ten years, many companies have launched Internet shopping-mall businesses.
  各位知道，過去十年來，許多公司都開始了網路商城事業。
- **You see**, it is a very lucrative business.
  各位知道，那是一個非常有利可圖的生意。
- **As a matter of fact**, in the last year alone, Internet shopping-mall sales have more than doubled.
  事實上，光是去年，網路商城的營業額就增加了一倍多。
- **Now**, it is time for us to start our own business.
  現在，該是開始我們的事業的時候了。
- **Then** what are we going to sell at the Internet shopping mall?
  那，我們應該在網路商城賣些什麼？
- **Well**, there is nothing we can't sell.
  嗯，沒有什麼我們不能賣的。
- **But**, to begin with, let us concentrate on selling our products, OK?
  不過，一開始先賣我們自己的產品吧，好嗎？
- **So**, let's increase our profits.
  所以，讓我們增加利潤吧。

隨堂測驗 A

1 off the top of my head 2 in a position to comment on that
3 as I talked about earlier 4 I don't see the connection.
5 What I'm saying is 6 I did not fully explain that

隨堂測驗 B

① Are there any ② as I said ③ a different issue ④ a position to answer
⑤ make you understand ⑥ If there are

Week 4 複習時間

A. 使用下面的單字完成句子。

afraid	mind	short	what
covers	that	summarizing	keep

1 ___________ my points, we need to develop a training program.
總結我的重點，我們需要開發一個教育課程。

2 In ___________, the introduction of the 6 Sigma Movement led to a 10% increase in productivity.
簡而言之，六標準差活動的採用讓產能增加了 10%。

3 Please ___________ the following recommendations in ___________.
請牢記以下的建議。

4 We have to close down the plants ___________ are not making a profit. That's ___________ this presentation is all about.
我們必須關閉不賺錢的工廠。這就是我簡報所要說的。

5 I'm ___________ I don't have the figures with me.
我恐怕並沒有確切的數據。

6 That ___________ all that I wanted to say today.
以上就是我今天想要說的。

B. 使用提示句完成下列句子。

1 在我結束之前，讓我再次強調為何需要撤出海外市場。

Hint Before ~, let me stress ~

→ ______________________________ from the overseas market.

2 最後我要重申，我們需要重新聚焦在線上事業上。

Hint I'd like to conclude by ~

→ ______________________________

3 抱歉，或許我剛才並沒有說得很清楚。

Hint not make ~ clear

→ Sorry, ______________________________

4 我要感謝史密斯先生特別從紐約前來。

Hint I'd like to / thank someone for -ing

→ ______________________________

5 如各位所見，有幾個非常好的理由。

Hint As + 主詞 + 動詞, there are~

→ ______________________________

6 我相信可以從這當中學到的教訓是很清楚明白的。

Hint I'm sure ~ is evident

→ I am sure ______________________________

C. 根據提示完成下面簡報的空格。 MP3 36

1

So, ladies and gentlemen, I would like to _______ today's presentation by _______ what I have been talking about. Three key elements should be considered in making a new MP3 player, which will be our flagship product. They are first, a user-friendly design, second, durability, and third, a competitive price.

Thank you very much for _______ _______. That brings me to _______ _______ of my presentation. Now, it is time for a question-and-answer session. _______ _______ any questions about my proposal?

所以，各位女士先生，我將做總結來結束本日的簡報。製造將會成為我們主力商品的新的 MP3 播放器需要考慮三個要素。第一是便於使用的設計，第二是耐用性，第三是有競爭力的價格。

感謝各位的聆聽，我的簡報到此結束。接下來是提問的時間。各位對我的提案有沒有任何問題？

2

A: Are there ①________ ________ or comments about the presentation I have made this morning?

B: I have a question.

A: Yes, please. ②________ ________.

B: I am not sure I understand the meaning of the word "ergonomics," which you used several times in your presentation.

A: I am very glad ③________ ________ ________. "Ergonomics" is the study of work, workers, and the working environment regarding efficiency, convenience, and safety. ④________ ________ ________ your question? (Yes.) Good. May ⑤________ ________ ________? Any other questions? … Yes, please.

C: I like your proposal that we need to design our product in such a way as to reflect ergonomics. But my question is, "Do we have design staff to deal with that area?"

A: 各位對我今早的簡報有任何問題或意見嗎？

B: 我有一個問題。

A: 好，請說。

B: 我不是很確定我了解「人體工學」這個詞的意思，你在簡報裡用過好幾次。

A: 很高興你問到這個。「人體工學」是一個研究工作、員工、以及工作環境相關的效率、便利性與安全性的學問。這樣有回答到您的問題嗎？（有）我們可以繼續嗎？有其他的問題嗎？……好，請。

C: 我很欣賞你簡報所說的要以能夠反映人體工學來設計產品。但是我的問題是，「我們有可以處理相關領域的設計員工嗎？」

A: ⑥________ ________ ________ very good question. Of course, we don't. I think we need outsourcing. That's all I can answer right now. Any ⑦________ ________ or comments? … Yes, please.

D: What kind of a future do you see for our product with regards to an ergonomical design?

A: If I understand you correctly, are you ⑧________ ________ to predict how many units we can sell a year?

D: Yes. It would be helpful if you used numbers.

A: I am afraid that is a ⑨________ ________ ________. Although I can't give you exact figures, I would say that the product will help us to get back to the black. Any other questions?

A: 這是一個非常好的問題。當然，我們沒有。我認為我們需要外包。這是我現在能做的回答。還有其他問題或意見嗎？……是，請。

D: 如果我們的產品符合人體工學，你認為後勢會是怎樣？

A: 如果我的理解正確的話，您是不是要我預測我們每年可以賣多少件？

D: 是的，如果你能提出數字的話會很有幫助。

A: 那是一個相當不好回答的問題。雖然我沒有辦法提出確切數字，但是我相信這個產品會幫助我們轉虧為盈。還有其他問題嗎？

E: Could you expand on what you said about your plan to improve our productivity?

A: I am sorry. Perhaps I did not make ⑩________ ________ ________.
⑪________ ________ ________ ________ to say was that we first need to upgrade our production facilities. And then we also need to help our staff to improve their job skills.

Have I made ⑫________ ________? Any other questions? If there are no other questions, why don't we ⑬________ ________ ________ here? I'd like to thank you all ⑭________ ________ ________ and contributions.

E: 可以請你多說明一下改善產能的計畫嗎？

A: 對不起，或許我剛才並沒有說得很清楚。我剛才想說的是我們首先要升級生產設備，然後還必須幫助員工改善他們的工作技能。

我這樣說夠清楚了嗎？還有其他問題嗎？如果沒有其他問題，我們何不就到此結束？我要感謝各位的參與和投入。

Answers

A 1 Summarizing 2 short 3 keep / mind 4 that / what 5 afraid 6 covers

B 1 Before I finish, let me stress why we must withdraw from the overseas market.
2 I'd like to conclude by repeating that we need to refocus on our online business.
3 Sorry, perhaps I did not make that quite clear.
4 I'd like to thank Mr. Smith for coming over from New York.
5 As you can see, there are some very good reasons.
6 I am sure the lessons to be learned from this are evident.

C 1 finish[end / conclude] / summarizing / your attention / the end / Are there
2 ① any questions ② Go ahead ③ you asked that ④ Did I answer[Does that answer] ⑤ we move[go] on ⑥ That is a ⑦ other questions ⑧ asking me ⑨ rather difficult question ⑩ that quite clear ⑪ What I was trying ⑫ that clear ⑬ wrap it up ⑭ for your participation

國家圖書館出版品預行編目(CIP)資料

上班族週末充電課：簡報英文／劉培均作.
-- 初版. -- 臺北市：貝塔, 2017. 06
面；　公分

ISBN: 978-986-94176-2-4（平裝）

1. 英語　2. 簡報　3. 會話

805.188　　106007432

上班族週末充電課：簡報英文

作　　者／劉培均
譯　　者／朱淯萱
執行編輯／朱曉瑩

出　　版／貝塔出版有限公司
地　　址／台北市 100 中正區館前路 12 號 11 樓
電　　話／(02) 2314-2525
傳　　真／(02) 2312-3535
客服專線／(02) 2314-3535
客服信箱／btservice@betamedia.com.tw
郵撥帳號／19493777
帳戶名稱／貝塔出版有限公司

總 經 銷／時報文化出版企業股份有限公司
地　　址／桃園市龜山區萬壽路二段 351 號
電　　話／(02) 2306-6842

出版日期／2017 年 6 月初版一刷
定　　價／320 元
I S B N／978-986-94176-2-4

貝塔網址：www.betamedia.com.tw

喚醒你的英文語感！

折後釘好，直接寄回即可！

廣　告　回　信
北區郵政管理局登記證
北台字第14256號
免　貼　郵　票

100 台北市中正區館前路12號11樓

貝塔語言出版 收

Beta Multimedia Publishing

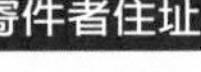

寄件者住址 □□□

貝塔語言出版
Beta Multimedia Publishing
讀者服務專線（02）2314-3535　讀者服務傳真（02）2312-3
客戶服務信箱 btservice@betamedia.com.tw
www.betamedia.com.tw

謝謝您購買本書！！

貝塔語言擁有最優良之英文學習書籍，為提供您最佳的英語學習資訊，您可填妥此表後寄回（免貼郵票）將可不定期收到本公司最新發行書訊及活動訊息！

姓名：＿＿＿＿＿＿＿＿＿＿　性別：□男 □女　生日：＿＿＿年＿＿＿月＿＿＿日

電話：(公)＿＿＿＿＿＿＿＿＿(宅)＿＿＿＿＿＿＿＿＿(手機)＿＿＿＿＿＿＿＿

電子信箱：＿＿＿＿＿＿＿＿＿＿＿＿＿＿＿＿＿＿＿＿

學歷：□高中職含以下　□專科　□大學　□研究所含以上

職業：□金融　□服務　□傳播　□製造　□資訊　□軍公教　□出版

□自由　□教育　□學生　□其他

職級：□企業負責人　□高階主管　□中階主管　□職員　□專業人士

1. 您購買的書籍是？＿＿＿＿＿＿＿＿＿＿＿＿＿＿＿

2. 您從何處得知本產品？(可複選)

□書店 □網路 □書展 □校園活動 □廣告信函 □他人推薦 □新聞報導 □其他

3. 您覺得本產品價格：

□偏高 □合理 □偏低

4. 請問目前您每週花了多少時間學英語？

□ 不到十分鐘 □ 十分鐘以上，但不到半小時 □ 半小時以上，但不到一小時

□ 一小時以上，但不到兩小時 □ 兩個小時以上 □ 不一定

5. 通常在選擇語言學習書時，哪些因素是您會考慮的？

□ 封面 □ 內容、實用性 □ 品牌 □ 媒體、朋友推薦 □ 價格□ 其他＿＿＿＿

6. 市面上您最需要的語言書種類為？

□ 聽力 □ 閱讀 □ 文法 □ 口説 □ 寫作 □ 其他＿＿＿＿＿

7. 通常您會透過何種方式選購語言學習書籍？

□ 書店門市 □ 網路書店 □ 郵購 □ 直接找出版社 □ 學校或公司團購

□ 其他＿＿＿＿＿＿

8. 給我們的建議：＿＿＿＿＿＿＿＿＿＿＿＿＿＿＿＿＿＿＿＿＿＿＿＿＿

＿＿＿＿＿＿＿＿＿＿＿＿＿＿＿＿＿＿＿＿＿＿＿＿＿＿＿＿＿＿＿＿＿＿＿

喚醒你的英文語感！

Get a Feel for English !